CALAMINE

CALAMINE

a novel

by
Mark Wyatt

BASED ON A SONG BY ROSS NEWELL

Wyatt House Publishing
Mobile, Alabama

Wyatt House books may be ordered through booksellers or by contacting:

Wyatt House Publishing
399 Lakeview Dr. W.
Mobile, Alabama   36609

Because of the dynamic nature of the Internet, any web address or links contained in this book may have changed since publication and may no longer be valid.

Cover design by: Mark Wyatt
Interior design by: Mark Wyatt

ISBN 13: 978-1-7345398-3-7

Printed in the United States of America

"People thought me bad before, but if ever I should get free, I'll let them know what bad means."

- Billy the Kid

CHAPTER 1

Maybe it was the sounds of her dying that made it feel so cold. Haddon wondered how he could shiver and be covered in sweat at the same time. He looked up at the window in the wall above him and watched as the thin curtain moved in the wind, like it was saying good-bye, too. She had hung that curtain for him. She liked the red ribbon across the bottom of it, said it added some much needed color to the room.

Even at ten years old, Haddon Chambers knew that you couldn't really see the wind it-self, only what it touched, but as he looked up at the window, he thought that must not be all the way true, because he saw the wind blowing in, blue and curling through the small opening at the bottom, and he thought it looked like fingers grabbing for—what? Her last breaths, maybe. The only thing left of her.

The door to Haddon's room, already standing ajar, creaked open some more as a tall man shuffled through, leathered by the elements and beaten down by everything and everyone else. He held a box, wrapped in green and red and taped by loving hands. It was one of the last things her hands did before they got too weak to move.

"Well," the man said, "Doctor says you're prob'ly gonna pull though this. Your Ma is nigh to death, though. That fever you brung in here's got a hold of her now. I told her not to get close to you. I told her to just let you go on. But she didn't never listen to me anyhow." He looked at the gift in his hands. "Your Ma told me to make sure you got this. Just as well. You got to start bein' a man some time. So. Here." The man went to set the box on Haddon's bedside table, but didn't make the effort to lean down the last few inches, so it landed with a muffled thump. He turned, and as he passed back through the doorway, said, over his shoulder, "Merry Christmas."

Haddon tried to sit up, but his body refused to obey him. He closed his eyes, took a deep breath, at least as deep as he could, and tried again. This time, he was just able to reach the box on the bedside table and slide it closer. He leaned back in bed, took a moment to let his strength gather again, and pulled the gift from the table onto his bed. He took his time unwrapping the box, not because he was weak from sickness, but because he knew this was the last gift he would ever receive from his mother. It needed to last.

The bright wrapping peeled away and revealed a plain wooden box underneath. Haddon carefully lifted the lid, and an aroma of oil and metal rose to greet him, transforming the air around him, and he thought he heard it call his name. With both hands, Haddon reached inside the box and lifted out the Colt .45 Single Action Army revolver. The wooden grip had been worn smooth by someone else's countless acts of bravery and action, and though the metal was dull in the fading light of the day, to Haddon it shone as if it had just been polished by Captain Bill McDonald himself. Haddon also knew that this gun was called the "Peacemaker," and he hoped that it would bring some kind of peace between he and his father.

Haddon turned the gun over in his hands and memorized its curves and shadows from every angle. He took the grip in both hands, raised it, and shut his left eye as he peered over the iron sights. The barrel was too heavy for him to keep lifted, so he let it sag down to the bed-covers, but he knew that he would handle it well when he was stronger.

Haddon was thinking about what it would sound like when he fired the Peacemaker, so he jumped inside his skin when a sharp rap banged above him. He looked up and saw the cold face of another boy, about his age, probably, wiping frost off the outside of the window. The boy's eyes searched the room before finding Haddon in the bed below the window. Haddon heard him say something, but it was too muffled to hear.

"What?" asked Haddon.

"Can I open it some more? This here window?"

Haddon nodded. "Okay." The boy grunted as he slid the window up further, high enough to stick his head in the room. Dark, windblown hair framed a face that was probably ruddy in the summertime, but in the cold of this Christmas Eve, his sharp nose and chin looked like chiseled marble, his eyes like two blue stones trapped inside of it.

"Hey," said the boy.

"Hey."

"You sick?"

"Yes," said Haddon.

"Bad sick?"

"Yeah, but getting better."

"Oh. Me and my Pa just settled a little ways from here. Wanted to see if any kids lived here. My name's Calamine."

"Mine's Haddon Chambers."

A fevered, pained moan pushed its way into Haddon's room from down the hall, followed by the gush of what he knew was black vomit. When that stopped, it was just a woman crying again.

"That's my Ma," said Haddon. "She's sick, too."

"Oh. She dying?"

"Yes."

Calamine nodded his head toward the Peacemaker. "That your gun?"

Haddon looked at it again as if it had just appeared in his lap for the first time. "Yes."

"That's a nice't un. Can you shoot?

"No."

"Well," said Calamine, "when you get better, I'll show you how. I'm pretty good. I'll be back when you're better, okay?"

Haddon nodded. "Okay."

Calamine slid the window back down to where it had been before, and Haddon heard his footsteps fade away, crunching on sticks and a dusting of snow.

His mother moaned once more, softer now, and then it was quiet. Her moan was replaced by a new sound, that of his father and brother crying, coming from that same place down the hall.

CHAPTER 2

Nine Years Later

The church is empty, save for one young man in a black suit. The suit had grown too small for his lanky frame a few years back, but there isn't money for a new one. He certainly hasn't gotten too fat for it, in fact it still hangs loose from his shoulders, but a good five inches of sock shows beneath each pant leg, and the sleeves ride halfway up to his elbows when he gestures, which he is wont to do. Haddon Chambers has the build of his father, but he hoped that was all that he carried of the bitter old man.

Haddon sits quietly on the front pew, staring forward for another moment, before he rises with dignity and steps to the oak podium in the shape of a cross. "I believe we will dispense with the hymn-singing today," he says, "and get right into the preaching of the Word of God." He flips his black leather Bible open to a book-marked place. "Our text today comes from the book of Proverbs, the 29th chapter and the 25th and 26th verses. 'The fear of man bringeth a snare: but whoso putteth his trust in the Lord shall be safe. Many seek the ruler's favor. But every man's judgment cometh from the Lord.'"

He looks around slowly at the empty pews, as the wind blows in the open windows and sways the hanging lights that are as dark and cold as he feels. Sadness passes quickly over his face on its way to resolve, then anger, without stopping in between. "And again," he says, and the words echo off the walls. "The Apostle Paul writes in First Corinthians chapter 4, in the fourth verse: "For I am conscious of nothing against myself, yet I am not by this acquitted; but he that judgeth me is the Lord!" Haddon's sermon only picks up speed and vigor from there, his long blonde hair becoming damp with Scripture and indignation.

Breakfast the next morning is, as usual for Monday, a somber affair. Then again, somber is the defining characteristic of the whole house every day, not just Mondays. Every bit of color and life and vibrance bled out of this place the night his mother died.

Haddon broods over his plate of eggs, a slab of salt ham, and a biscuit, moving them around more than eating them. Then the day grows a little darker when his father speaks. Joseph Chambers is sitting by the back door, putting his boots back on, since he has already been up and at work on the farm for three hours. Haddon is glad that he is leaving again.

"Well boy," says his father, "I can't say as I blame those folk. I mean, folks don't always like to listen to a preacher from the next town over, one that a lot of 'em knew growin' up. They done seen all his thorns and thistles."

Haddon looks at a bowl of grits that his stepmother placed behind him. He takes a spoon and stirs it with great thought. "'Is this not Joesph's son?'"

Joseph Chambers perks up and squints at Haddon. "What's that?"

"Nothing. Just something they said about Jesus."

Joseph grunts as he pulls his other boot on and says, "Well, you ain't Jesus, that's for damn sure."

Haddon stares at his father for a moment, trying to count all of the unnecessary wounds that have been inflicted on him at this table.

"Still," he says, "I don't think that's why they all stopped coming over the course of two months."

"What do you think it was, sweetheart?" Haddon's stepmother speaks softly behind him. She does everything soft, it seems to him. She has been his father's wife since a year after Haddon's mother died, and she seems to think herself lucky to have found a good provider. Haddon supposes she has nothing to gain by rocking this decaying boat. Besides, she knows her husband's temper, which makes speaking her mind about anything risky. Haddon doesn't expect encouragement from anyone, so it surprises him a little when she says, even lower than a moment ago, "You know that if I could stand the horse or carriage ride that far, I would be there every single Sunday, I swanee I would, I hope you know that. It's just my tailbone, you know how..."

"I know, Abigail. It's alright.

Joseph pauses long enough to bite into the atmosphere again. "I'll tell you every time, call her 'mother,' boy."

"Now, Joseph, he doesn't have to call me that."

"He does if I say he does."

For the first time, as if just appearing in the room like a ghost, his brother speaks from the doorway. "Why'd they stop coming, Haddon?"

Haddon looks at him with the calm that goes alongside explaining to a child how the sun rises and sets. "I think it's clear, Ethan. They just can't take hearing the truth about themselves. For a while, they came to me with their questions and problems, but I swear, it was like dealing with idiots, and I told them so. Mr. Heller wants to know why his wife left, and I told him it was probably because he got drunk and hit her every night. Mrs. Watson asks me to pray over her garden, but I don't have power over God, and I told her so. And Mrs. Daughtry wants me to court her granddaughter, but there's a reason no one has courted her yet. She's twice as mean as she is ugly, so I told her that, too."

Joseph shakes his head, laughs, coughs up phlegm, and spits it out the door. "Damn, boy. I don't think I'd show up to hear you, either. And I don't think I'll be askin' your opinion about anything any time soon." With that, Joseph rises, nods to Ethan, and the two step back out into the workday of a real man.

Haddon frowns and rolls a cigarette at the farmhouse table. "I could have helped Daddy and Ethan out there."

"I know you think you could," says Abigail, "but it's best not to chance it.

"I haven't been sick for a long time."

"Maybe not, but you were weak for a long time, too. You're just not as strong as your brother, you know that."

"Yes, I do know that. How can I not know it, when everybody tells me."

"Now, you know I didn't meant it like that..."

"I don't mean you so much," says Haddon. "Everybody else, though. 'Ethan's a right good farmer now, ain't he?' 'That Ethan's a fine lookin' young man, now, ain't he?' 'How you doin', Haddon? You feelin' alright? You could sure use a haircut.'"

Haddon watches Abigail's back at the sink, hoping she will turn and tell him he's wrong. Then again, she's heard it all before. What is there that's new to say? "Maybe," Haddon continues, "those people from the church want somebody from a seminary. Maybe I'm not educated enough for them." This makes Abigail whirl around.

"My Lord, Haddon, you read more than anybody I've ever seen. You have educated yourself. Goodness, just think about your name, Wesley Haddon Chambers. Your mama named you after two great preachers, John Wesley and Charles Haddon Spurgeon. That right there ought to be enough of the calling of God on you for anybody. Don't you worry. They'll come

18

around and they'll come back, and that church house will be full in a month."

Haddon strikes a match, holds it up to the cigarette, and takes a long pull. "They better," he said. "I can't go on through the rest of my life feeling like a pretender at everything and good at nothing."

CHAPTER 3

The next Sunday morning, empty oak pews are still the only hearers in the old white clapboard church, but like before, Haddon won't let a little thing like that keep him from proclaiming his message. "Today," he says, "I am going to speak on a subject that many people have need of hearing, if only they could stomach truth when it is spoken. I am going to take my text today from the 1881 English Revised Version of the Scriptures, because I believe that it states more plainly what needs to be shouted from the rooftops. Our text is found in Proverbs..."

The back door opens, not much, but enough to let in a young man who looks to be about Haddon's own age. He walks softly down the aisle, sits on the front pew, and settles in to listen.

"In Proverbs," Haddon continues, "the 18th chapter and the 24th verse. Here the wise King Solomon says, 'He that maketh many friends doeth it to his own destruction: but there is a friend that sticketh closer than a brother.'"

"Amen," says the stranger.

Haddon is encouraged by this small "amen corner", and goes on. "I believe it is incumbent on us," he says, "to have to walk through this weary world with others at our side, even if we sometimes may feel that we would do better to traverse alone. No, it cannot be so. And yet, as Solomon points out here, a myriad of friends can lead to one's own destruction. According to Solomon, all we really need is one good one."

"Amen, sir," says the stranger again. "Amen."

Almost an hour later, Haddon and the young man walk out of the front doors together and Haddon turns to lock them. "I appreciate your coming today, mister," he says, "and your kind listening."

"Oh," says the man, "that wasn't no act of kindness, Reverend…"

"You don't have to…" interrupts Haddon. "I mean, I'm not a Reverend. I haven't been to theology school or anything. I'm not ordained."

"Allow me to disagree, sir," says the man. "I just heard one of the greatest sermons of my life, and I'd say you were greatly ordained by God Hisself to preach. If you'll pardon my saying so."

Haddon smiles at the first kind words he has heard since he can remember. "Well, again, I appreciate it. I am Haddon Chambers, by the way."

"Yessir," says the stranger. "I know you."

Haddon frowns as he tries to recall. "Have we met?"

"Met? Hell, we were friends. I'm Calamine."

"What?" says Haddon. "Calamine! How long has it been? Seven or eight years, I guess?"

"Yes, sir, about that, I reckon."

Another thought comes to Haddon. "I am sorry I didn't recognize you." Then Haddon sees in his eyes the boy who looked into his frost-covered window that coldest of Christmas Eves.

"Well," says Calamine, "I got more miles on me than years. Tends to change a man somewhat."

Haddon extends his hand to his old friend. "Well, Calamine, I'm headed home. See you next Sunday?"

Calamine shakes his hand, and his grip is firm. Haddon starts to pull his hand back but Calamine holds tight. "You sure will," he says. His eyes lock onto Haddon's. "And just so you know, I agree with everything you said in there, Rev—I mean, Haddon. You only need one good friend. And sometimes that friend is closer to you than your own brother. Sometimes even a brother don't stand by you like he should." Calamine keeps his grip tight and pulls Haddon in closer to him, close enough for Haddon to feel Calamine's breath, musty and damp. "'This," he says, "'is what the LORD, the God of Israel, says: "Each man strap a sword to his side. Go back and forth through the camp from one end to the other, each killing his brother and friend and neighbor."' Exodus 32:27."

Calamine releases Haddon's hand, steps back, tips his hat, then turns and walks away into the nearby woods. Haddon stares after him until he is gone, a little bewildered, but grateful for the conversation. Then he turns, cinchs his saddle, mounts up, and heads for home.

The East Texas night air is beginning to come with a chill on the breeze as autumn announces her soon arrival. Ethan Chambers is finishing his last task of the day as the light in the sky turns from pink to purple on the horizon, and he knows that soon it will be too dark to see. He has to get this fencepost repaired and the barbed wire restrung back to the other side of the creek before that happens. He kneels at the post, making sure it is firmly planted in the ground, when he hears the crack of a twig in the trees in front of him.

"Daddy?" he says. "Is that you?"

As he turns and stands, he barely has time to see an arm raised in his direction, with a long-barreled revolver in the hand at the end of it. Before he can finish opening his mouth, the black hole of the barrel explodes, and Ethan is never even aware of his body twisting and falling facedown in the shallow water, or of the footsteps of his killer splashing back the way they had come.

Haddon is still in bed when the usual morning calm is shattered by a mournful, agonized wail. He remembers that wail. He has only heard it once before. And just like last time, it is coming from his father.

Haddon runs from his room and rounds the corner into the kitchen to see his brother's body laid out on the kitchen table. Ethan's skin is pale and waxy, and Haddon can tell right away that the back of his brother's head is gone. There is one round hole in the middle of his forehead. Joseph Chambers is lying over the body of his dead son, sobbing. Abigail sits weeping in a chair in the corner of the room. Ben Simmons, the local sheriff, is standing just outside the room, head bowed, and hat in his hands.

"Daddy?" Haddon says.

His father doesn't look up. "Just look at my boy," he chokes out.

"What happened?" Haddon says. "What happened to Ethan?"

Joseph lifts himself off of Ethan's body enough to speak. "Found him like this, face down in Thrush Creek this morning. Brung him back here."

"When?" cries Haddon. "When did this happen? I didn't hear anything!"

Joseph looks at him and through him at the same time. "Some time last night, I reckon. He went out near dark to check on a section of fence on the other side of the creek. I shouldn't have went to sleep without him here."

Sheriff Simmons speaks from the doorway. "Ain't your fault, Joseph. He was a grown man. Nothing you could've done."

"How come you're here so fast, Mr. Simmons?" says Haddon. "Do you have any idea who did this?"

"No, Haddon," he says, "I don't. "Your Daddy rode right by my place on the way back here and I came with him. I need to ask you something, though."

"Go ahead," says Haddon. Somehow he knows what's coming.

"Where was you last night, Haddon?"

"In my room," says Haddon. "Reading."

"Don't suppose anybody else saw you here?"

No," says Haddon, "I can't prove it, if that's what you're asking."

"Hold on, son," says Simmons. "There's nothing to prove yet...

Joseph stands up straight. "The hell there ain't! You did this, boy, and you and me both know it! You was jealous of your brother because he was the good one and you wished you was half the man he was! You went out there and put a bullet in his head with that .45 I give you for Christmas! You killed your own brother, the son of your mother, with a gift you got for Christmas!"

Haddon looks to Abigail, but she just buries her face deeper into her handkerchief and weeps harder. "Daddy," he says, "I haven't done anyth—"

"Don't you ever call me that again! Don't ever call me your Daddy! Get out of here, boy, " he says through gritted teeth. "Leave here. I will not stand to let this town see your dead Mama's own son hang, but I'll be damned if you will breathe another lungful of air under my roof!"

Haddon moves his mouth to speak, but nothing comes out. Joseph speaks again, with a quietness so loud it threatens to shatter the sky. *"Leave."*

Sheriff Simmons steps over to Haddon and takes him gently by the arm. "Let's go outside, son," he says. "Come on." Haddon allows himself to be led out the back door, walking too close to Ethan's body. When they are well outside, Simmons speaks again. "Well," he says, "What do you have to say for yourself?

Haddon is still in a daze. "How's that?"

Simmons looks at him without blinking. "Did you do this?"

"No!" Haddon says. "God, no!" And as the words hang in the air, a memory flashes into Haddon's mind: Calamine. *Sometimes even a brother don't stand by you like he should... This is what the LORD, the God of Israel, says: 'Each man strap a sword to his side... each killing his brother...*

Haddon feels a certain resolve growing in the darkness of his fog. "Are you arresting me, sheriff?" he says.

"No, Haddon," says Simmons. "Nothing like that. But I'm gonna have to look closer, you know that. Sad to say, it's the only thing that makes sense right now. I got nobody else to question."

Haddon turns in the direction of the church. "I do," he says.

CHAPTER 4

Haddon rides up fast and dismounts before his horse has come to a stop. He throws open the front door and stalks inside. There, on the front pew, facing the pulpit as if he expects someone to start preaching, sits Calamine, black hair slicked back, hands in his lap. Calamine speaks without turning around.

"Morning, preacher. I thought I might stand a good chance of running into you here today," he says.

Haddon strides to the front, fists balled, and stands over Calamine. "What did you do?"

"Sorry?"

"What did you *do*!?"

"Well. I've done lots of things."

Haddon grabs Calamine by the collar and tries to stand him up, but he isn't strong enough.

Calamine shakes his head and stands up in front of him. "Whoa, there, preacher," he says, "'An angry man stirreth up strife, and a furious man aboundeth in transgression.' Proverbs 29:22."

Haddon releases Calamine's bunched up shirtfront from his fists, but doesn't step back. "Tell me about Ethan!"

Calamine begins to walk a slow circle around Haddon. "What do you want to know that you don't already? He was better than you in every way, and you were *never* going to feel the sun outside of his shadow. I believe that you can be a great man, Haddon, but you got to start deciding some things."

Haddon collapses onto the front pew, exhausted and wrung out by emotion. "You didn't have to kill him," he said.

Calamine kneels in front of him. "You ain't listening, preacher. I'm not saying I did anything. You're just assuming things. Fact is, if I am not mistaken, the long arm of the law just might be pointing its bony finger at you right about now."

Haddon slumps forward and puts his face in his hands. "Jesus," he says.

Calamine sits on the pew next to Haddon and bows his head. "Amen," he says. He stands again, smooths his shirt, and clears his throat. "Now, seems to me," he says, "you got some thinkin' to do, so I will let you get to it. But I will say this, Haddon Chambers. The way I see it, you are free right now. Really free. Free to prove that you are the man I know you are, free to prove everyone wrong. You have the chance, right now, to leave this place and start a real life. But, I assure you, if you sit here on your Blessed Assurance too long, the people of this community are going to see to it that somebody pays for your brother, and don't nobody around here even know who I am. So I suggest you get to moving."

Calamine walks down the aisle to the back door, then he turns to Haddon. "If," he says, "you are having trouble with this predicament, though, I would like to suggest one more thing, if I may. You remember Old Mr. Spragg? You've heard of him, I know. Everybody here has. Lives out past the north ridge. Some folks say that demons talk to him, others say he hears God. Either way, he might have a message for you, whether from hell or from heaven." Calamine shrugs. "Just a thought. I mean, you might as well. Not like you can go home now, is it? You have a good day, now, Preacher Haddon." Calamine walks out and leaves Haddon staring at the closing door.

Haddon leaves the building, his mind spinning. He mounts his horse and starts for home, the direction he always takes. Then he pulls on the reins until his horse comes to a stop. He sits there, deciding, as the horse paws the ground, eager to move. After a few long moments, Haddon looks left—to the north—and spurs his horse forward in that direction.

Haddon rides hard for some time, stopping only to water his horse at a stream or let her eat hay in a field or by the side of the road. The sun moves through its zenith at noon, then it keeps going. He and the horse can rest later. Finally, it is sinks behind the treetops of the East Texas pines when he makes his way up the north ridge toward a simple house, built up off the ground, a decaying porch on the front of it.

Some might say the house has seen better days, but there is some question as to whether it ever had any good ones at all. Vines weave in and out of the places where wall meets roof, and it seems that the surrounding trees are only waiting for the place's sole tenant to die so they can reclaim this small piece of land.

As Haddon dismounts and leads the horse to a nearby bucket of water, the only sign of life is a yellow hound asleep on the top step of the porch, its eyes regarding Haddon's approach. As Haddon puts a foot on the bottom step, the dog stands. Haddon pauses, giving the dog time to assess him. The hound looks him over, snuffles in his direction, then turns and lumbers into the partially open front door. A voice speaks from the darkness inside.

"Best come in, son," it says. "You ain't gonna get nowhere in life by standin'."

Haddon steps inside like a latecomer to a funeral, and sees a man standing at the fireplace, stirring a pot of stew. His hair and beard are both gray, but not unruly, though a little long. He turns to Haddon, and his skin is dark and deep, and cracked like saddle leather that hasn't been oiled in a long time. But he is not stooped or weakened with age. As Haddon's vision adjusts to the dim light of the room, he sees that the pupils in both of the man's eyes are milky white.

"Mr. Spragg?" says Haddon.

"I am," says the old man.

"My name is Haddon Chambers. I was told... I just...I thought maybe you could help me."

"Why?"

"Sir?"

"Why'd you think I could help you?"

Haddon thinks for a moment. "I... I'm not sure."

"Hmph," says the man. "I get that a lot. Sit down, son, anywhere you like."

Haddon moves to a tattered floral wingback

chair and turns to sit down. Spragg looks like he is still staring at the front door.

"Not there," says Spragg.

Haddon freezes. "I'm sorry?"

"I said, not there. Dadgum, boy, am I gonna have to repeat everything? If so, I might have to take a nap before we start talking. Reserve some strength."

"Uh, no, sir," says Haddon, "you won't have to... No, sir." Haddon looks at the chair behind him. "How did you know...?"

Spragg nods and moves to the wingback chair, where he settles in. Haddon sits on a horsehide couch facing him. "Just because I'm blind, don't mean I can't see," he says.

"I thought that was exactly what it meant," says Haddon.

"Shows what you know. There's more than one way of seeing."

"Maybe you can find a way to help me."

"Well," says Spragg, "we'll see." He smiles. "That's a joke."

Haddon stares into the distance, not knowing how to begin. The old man interrupts the silence. "As it happens," he says, "another thing I can *'see'* is that you don't even know why you're here. I get that a lot, too. So let me help you. I know who you are. I know what's happened last night, too. That ain't nothing special to know, though. I got a cousin comes round every day to see me, makes sure I have what I need. He told me. Whole region knows by now, I suppose. Anyhow, I know."

Haddon hangs his head, exhausted in every way that a man can be. He looks at Mr. Spragg. "Can you help me?" he says.

"Help you how?"

Haddon is too tired to figure out a riddle. "I don't know! That's why I came... Why did I even..."

Old man Spragg breaks in. "Hold out your hands, son."

"Why?"

"Just hold 'em out, like you're about to receive a gift."

Slowly, Haddon extends his hands, face up, until they are halfway between the two men. Like the strike of a snake, Spragg grabs his hands and grips them in a vise as strong and cold as steel. Haddon tries to pull them back, but he can't. Spragg's white eyes bore straight into Haddon's own, as if he is examining the nothingness in the deepest part of Haddon's soul. When the old man speaks, it was as if his voice is coming from somewhere else.

"'And the Lord said unto Cain, Why art thou angry? and why is thy countenance fallen? If thou doest well, shalt thou not be accepted? and if thou doest not well, sin lieth like a wolf at the door...'" Haddon doesn't like where this is headed, and opens his mouth to say so, but Old Mr. Spragg goes on. "'And Cain talked with Abel his brother: and it came to pass, when they were in the field, that Cain rose up against Abel his brother, and slew him. And the Lord said unto Cain, Where is Abel thy brother?'"

"Wait," says Haddon. "Why are you saying these things? What are you—"

"'...And he said, 'What hast thou done? The voice of thy brother's blood crieth unto me from the ground.'"

Haddon is stuck midway between paralysis and flight. Spragg's voice grows quieter, like a fit is passing.

"'...thy brother's blood crieth unto me from the ground.'" The old man releases Haddon's hands, sits back in the chair, and sighs. After a moment, his head turns toward the fireplace. "Gotta stir the stew," he says.

Haddon and Spragg sit at the table, a bowl of stew in front of each of them, a plate of bread in the middle. Spragg blows on a spoonful of stew and slurps it in. "Tell me about the wolf," he says.

"What wolf is that?" says Haddon.

"The one that's crouching at the door. That wolf."

Haddon knows exactly what—or whom—he means. "His name is Calamine."

Spragg frowns. "Calamine? Hm."

"That's all I know. I mean, I knew him as a boy, but that was a long time ago and I haven't seen him in years. Then he showed up at church last week. He is the only one who will come to hear me preach. Anyway, I think he's the one who shot Ethan. In fact, I'm sure of it."

"So tell somebody."

"I don't think I can. I don't know if anyone else knows he's here. So, right now, I am the prime suspect."

Spragg nods and takes another spoonful. "Yes," he says, "that you are."

Something about the old man's tone causes anxiety to well up deep in Haddon's chest. He looks around the room as the hair on his scalp tingled. "What are you doing?" he says. "Is this a trap? Are they coming here to arrest me?"

Old Mr. Spragg chuckles as he blows on a spoonful of stew. "Calm down boy," he says, "ain't nobody comin' to get you. No bounty on you. At least not yet." His smile grows wider. He takes a bite of stew. "So, the wolf, this Calamine. He do your bidding?"

"What?" said Haddon. "No! Of course not!"

Spragg shakes his head a little. "What I mean," he says, "is does he want to please you? Make you happy?"

Haddon thinks for a moment. "I'm not sure. I get the feeling I'm his only friend, and I think he sees himself as my protector of sorts. I didn't bring any of this on myself."

Spragg blows on another spoonful of stew. "Surely, you did," he says.

"Why would you say that?

"Because the wolf showed up, crouching at your door. 'If thou doest not well, sin lieth like a wolf at the door.' Apparently, you 'did not well.'"

Haddon reaches out and tears off a piece of bread. "I have no idea what I could have done," he says.

"You don't have to exactly know it," says the old man. "Mostly, the wolf sneaks in real quiet. But it comes to what it's hungry for. See, the wolf, it feeds on certain things. Jealously. Pride. Anger. Murder that's already in the heart."

"I did not murder my brother!"

"Not saying you did. But you let the wolf in, son. He done the rest."

He is moving through the woods, but no sound betrays his progress. Ghostlike, up the front steps, past the sleeping dog and into the house. Haddon is curled up on the couch, covered by a threadbare blanket, head on a thin cushion, stockinged feet sticking out from the blanket. The presence moves into the next room over, pushing through a wooden door, to where Old Man Spragg is snoring softly in his bed. A hand reaches out, the barrel of a gun a fraction of an inch from the blind man's head. The trigger finger tightens and the gun explodes.

Haddon bolts awake at the sound and runs into Spragg's room. "No!" he screams. "Calamine, what have you done!"

Spragg stirs from his sound sleep and lifts his head off of his pillow. "What in hell are you yellin' about, boy?" he slurs. "It's the middle of the damn night!"

Haddon tries to catch his breath and catch up with reality at the same time. "Calamine... I thought Calamine..."

The old man swings his legs out of the bed and stands. He puts both hands on Haddon's shoulders and squeezes, as he locked his blind eyes onto Haddon's seeing ones again. "It's time for you to run, friend," he says.

"I don't understand," says Haddon. "Run from what? Run where?

"You got to run from the wolf, boy. He ain't at the door anymore, he's walking around. Calamine is not your friend, son. The best thing you can do is leave. Run fast and run far. Find some pissant little town that nobody knows exists, and be somebody you want to be. You think nobody really sees you, I know that. But what'd I tell you about seeing?" The old man leans in closer. "I see you, son. You got to get far, far away from the wolf and what he feeds on. Start over somewhere and be the man that you always wanted everybody to see. Be who I see in you."

Haddon takes Mr. Spragg's hands from his shoulders, gives them a gentle squeeze in gratitude, gathers his suit coat, hat, and holster, and takes the old man's advice. He runs.

As Haddon mounts his horse, Spragg appears in the doorway, barely visible in the moonlight through the tree branches. "One more thing, friend," he says. Know this. No matter where you hide, the wolf will eventually find you. He will show his teeth again. Your only hope is that you have been somebody else long enough that you don't need him anymore. When that day comes—and it will come—don't feed the wolf, son. Whatever you do, for God's sakes, don't feed the wolf."

CHAPTER 5

Haddon Chambers arrives at his boyhood home just before light, knowing that his father will be up and headed out to his chores soon. It's been less than twenty-four hours since the old man wept over the body of his firstborn son laid out on the kitchen table, but Haddon knows him. The farming won't wait, and Ethan won't be back. So, just like every other morning, Joseph Chambers will do what must be done.

Sure enough, with just a little sunrise to see by, the kitchen door swings open and the lanky old man trudges out, milk pails in either hand. Haddon watches from the shadows of the house still hidden in the night, but there is enough light to see the changes in his father's face. The wrinkles are deeper, the frown burrowed deeper. There is pain there that will never go away.

When Haddon hears the barn door shut, he quietly slides through the kitchen door and down the short hallway to his bedroom. As gently as possible, he slides open the top drawer of his dresser, and chooses a few clothes, doesn't really matter what, he just has to get something. He reaches for the old Bible there, hesitates, then draws his hand back. Somehow it just feels wrong to leave it, and wrong to take it at the same time.

From the top of his dresser, Haddon lifts the old Colt .45 that his mother gave him for Christmas on her last day. He shines it a little with his sleeve, grabs the gun belt and bullets that he hasn't used in years, and stuffs it all into a canvas bag. He steps silently back down the hall and outside to his horse, and ties the sack to the saddle.

"Will I ever see you again?"

Haddon turns toward the soft voice and sees his stepmother in the doorway, her arms crossed, not in anger, but gathering her nightclothes to her against the pre-dawn cold. Haddon turns back to the saddle. "I don't know," he says.

"I know it wasn't you, Haddon." Her voice breaks with tears. "I know it wasn't you who killed him."

Haddon clutches the sack, nothing to say.

"But I forgive you," she says.

Haddon is suddenly infuriated, and the energy catapults him into the stirrup and into the saddle, where he looks down on her.

"Forgive me? Forgive *me*? For *what*?"

She looks up at him and smiles, forced and sad. "I know it wasn't you," she says. Then she turns, fades back into the darkness of the house, and closes the door.

Haddon's route out of town takes him past the church, and he shakes his head as he tries to resist the pull toward it. He gives the reins a feeble tug in the opposite direction, but his horse thinks that's where they are going, and it simply turns its massive head and trots up the road.

There is no one else at the church. There never is. Haddon notices a chain and padlock on the door. News has traveled, and somebody doesn't want him there, but that just makes him more determined to do what he had already decided against. He has to go in.

Haddon takes his .45 revolver, and after making sure that it is unloaded, he uses the handle like a hammer and breaks the old padlock with one blow. It is rusty and out of date, just something that had been laying around an old workshop for years. The church isn't even worth somebody's best lock.

Haddon walks past the pews, redolent with old pine and years of varnish. They are empty, of course, just like his heart. If they had been full when he needed them to be, his heart would be full, too. He sits in the third pew from the front, on the left side, and looks at the pulpit, seeing himself preaching with fire and passion, the church full of enraptured faces and grateful voices. But, in the silence, he only sees the absent faces turn toward him in disgust, wondering who he is and what gives him the right.

Haddon looks around at those faces with his own scorn, then stands and makes his way behind the pulpit. An old, tattered Bible is still there, as if consecrating the place, trying its best to ward off the evil. He begins to preach.

"Habakkuk, chapter 1, beginning in verse 8: 'Their horses are swifter than leopards, and are more fierce than the evening wolves; They come all of them for violence; their faces are set eagerly as the east wind; and they gather captives as the sand... for they shall heap dust, and take it.'" He looks up, searching for the listeners who are not there. "Ladies and gentlemen... You decide for yourselves what that means. As of today, I am no longer your pastor."

He steps down off the low platform and holds his head high as he walks past the ghosts of those who should have been there. And, in his heart, he knows that they are truly sad to see him go, for he was, by God, the best preacher they ever heard.

Haddon walks through the doors for the last time, and as he approaches his horse, Calamine steps around from the other side of the animal. "My goodness, Haddon," he says, "that was a hell of a sermon. Best I ever heard. Loud and clear, even out here in the yard."

"What are you doing here?"

"I always found you here before. Just waited. And here you are. I knew you wouldn't leave without me."

Haddon swings smoothly up into the saddle. "You're not coming."

"Well, you see," says Calamine, "I am. You need me, Haddon Chambers, and we both know it. I won't cause any trouble. Unless we meet trouble."

Haddon looks away, snaps the reins, and spurs his horse away, picking up speed as he goes down the road. A hundred yards along, he chances a glance behind him and sees Calamine, following on a horse of his own. A black one.

Haddon rides silently, no destination in mind, just west. He knows that Calamine has caught up and is riding a few yards behind, but neither of them tries to fill the silence with conversation. They make their way across the landscape and watch as the piney woods of east Texas give way to smaller trees, more scrub brush. As the tress get shorter, the sky gets larger, no longer blocked by the giants who ruled the woods around Haddon's memories. Haddon finds it strangely refreshing, and he takes a deep breath of the air of what could be a new life. But it's getting on dark, and he knows he has to stop, and he will, at the town coming up on the near horizon.

As the afternoon sun glows lower in the sky, Haddon—with Calamine behind him—rides past a wooden road sign that says, *Birthright, Texas. Population 233*. As they get closer, Haddon can see that Birthright looks to be home to a Post Office, a bank, two churches, a Sheriff's office, and most importantly right now, a hotel with a saloon.

After a few more minutes, Haddon and Calamine approach the hotel, slide off their horses, and walk up the steps to the entrance. Haddon has not realized how thirsty he is until he sees the glasses of beer on the tables in front of the scattered patrons of the hotel's ground floor saloon. As he walks to the bar, he sees that Calamine has claimed an empty table for the two of them.

"One beer, please," Haddon says.

The bartender pulls a draught into a pint glass, Haddon pays for it, and takes it to the table. "If you want anything," he says to Calamine, "you'll have to pay for it yourself. I'm almost out of money."

"Well," says Calamine, "that sounds like something we need to do something about."

"Getting you a beer?"

"No sir, I'm fine, thank you. I mean getting you some money."

Haddon takes a long draw, wipes the foam from his face, and shakes his head. "I'm not planning on being here long enough to take a job on somebody's farm, or ranch, or in some mercantile store. I'd rather keep moving."

"Oh, so would I," says Calamine. "I wasn't thinking of any of those things. I had something else in mind."

Haddon knows better than to ask what he's about to ask, but he knows there is no stopping himself, either. "And what would that be?"

Calamine leans in. "Haddon, didn't you notice the name of this town?

"Yes."

"Birthright," says Calamine.

"And?"

"Think back on your Bible stories, Mr. Preacher Man. Jacob and Esau?"

"Where are you going with this, Calamine?"

"Hear me out. Two twins. Jacob, just because he was a couple seconds coming out of their mother's womb behind his brother, is about to see his no 'count big, brawny, smelly brother inherit everything that he knows, by real rights, because he's smarter, you see, should be going to him."

"I know the story."

"Then think about it with me for another minute. Jacob, the younger, smarter, more ambitious one, tired of being in his brother's shadow, tricks their father into giving *him* the blessing. He gets it all and it can't be un-given, even when the deception is found out." Calamine pauses for a moment. "What town did you grow up in?"

"What?"

"The name of the town we come from. What was it?"

Haddon answers quietly, as if he has to force the words out like dry spit. "Black Ankle."

"How's that?"

"I said, Black Ankle."

"Say it louder."

In a moment, all of the pain and frustration

associated with the place surge through Haddon's soul and come rushing out of his body. He grips his beer glass almost to the point of breaking, glares at Calamine, and shouts it. "Black Ankle, Texas!"

Heads turn. Haddon lowers his head and his voice and stares into his glass. He looks sideways at Calamine. "What is your point?" he says.

"My point, Haddon, is that you don't see what you have been given, right here. Jacob means 'heel snatcher.' Like he gave his big brother a black ankle coming out of the womb." Calamine leans back in his chair and looks around the saloon. "This is it, Reverend Wesley Haddon Chambers. This is the time and place to claim your birthright." He spreads his arms wide. "Behold your inheritance!"

Haddon looks around, his brow furrowed. "I don't follow," he says.

Calamine shakes his head and leans forward again. "Then let me be clear," he says. "There is a bank across the street. First Bank of Birthright. Don't get no clearer than that, my friend."

Haddon shakes his head and laughs at the thought. Heads turn again. He leans closer to Calamine, and with a hard whisper, says, "We are not robbing a bank!"

"No, sir," says Calamine. "We are not robbing a bank."

Then what are you talking about?"

Calamine grins. "Like I said, we are not robbing a bank. We are robbing a *banker*."

"I can't do that," says Haddon.

Calamine nods. "I know. But like it or not, I'm going to. So, you best be outside of the bank with our horses at ten o'clock, or it's all gonna come down on your head."

Haddon stiffens his back. "You can't make me a party to this. I'll just turn you in!"

Calamine speaks gently, like he would talk to a child. "Yessir, you could. But then they might start looking at you, and find out that you skipped out of Black Ankle right after being questioned about your brother's murder. You really want that?"

Haddon can feel his breath getting shallow. He looks quickly around the room just to make sure the walls aren't closing in on him. "Alright," he says. "But if something goes wrong, I am leaving. Fast, and without you."

Calamine nods his agreement. "I can guarantee that ain't gonna happen. But it's a deal."

The night is of two minds. The moon is full and bright, but dark clouds skid across its face at uneven intervals, so that everything is either lit like daytime or swallowed by shadows, with no indication which way the next few seconds might take it. The bullfrogs are confused by it, the air filled with a racket one minute, then silent as a new grave the next.

Calamine stands at the edge of the tree line, nothing visible except the tips of his boots in the passing moon and the glint of dull metal as it twirls in his hand. He watches the house for a full minute more, then, satisfied that everyone is asleep, he makes his way over the soft grass, up a few steps, to the back door.

Birthright is a small town with trusting people, and Calamine just knows in his knower that these are the kind of people who don't lock their doors, even at night. They will tomorrow, though, and for quite a long time after that, he considers.

Calamine turns the knob on the back door and it softly squeaks as it obeys him without resistance. He steps into the kitchen just as the clouds give way and light up the porch behind him. Even as he moves through the bottom floor, he seems to always know when and where to go so that he is always in shadow. Calamine knows how to wear the night like a shroud, and it never exposes him. He stands at the bottom of the stairs and listens.

Calamine had watched the entrance of the First Bank of Birthright as it closed and followed the banker here, to his home. It was only a matter of waiting until he and his wife went to bed, which they did about nine o'clock. He counted the chimes as the lights went out behind them through the house. Now he cocks his head to the side a little, tuning his ears to the drone of sleep. There it is. The banker is snoring. Or could be his wife. You never know. He walks up the steps as quick and quiet as a cat. He wouldn't really care if he did make some noise, though. This would be over in just a second.

The bedroom door stands wide, apparently to aid a cross breeze from the window. The banker's wife lies on her side, facing Calamine as he walked in. She doesn't hear the slight rustle of his shirt sleeve as he raises his revolver and slams it down into the side of her head. Her breath huffs out of her once, but she stays quiet and still.

The motion and sound interrupts her husband's sleep, though, and he raises his head and says with a voice full of sleep, "Margaret, what—"

Calamine brings the hammer back with a click. "Now don't you go bothering Margaret, Mr. Banker. Me and you got business, and she don't never need to know. If I was you, I'd just leave her be."

The banker's eyes are wide and jittery, and he looks at the dark stain of blood on his wife's pillow. "Oh my god! What did you do? Who—"

Calamine pats the air with his other hand. "Just keep calm, stay quiet. I ain't gonna hurt you. I just need you to get out of bed and come with me."

"Come with you? Where?"

"Well, sir—you're going to work."

CHAPTER 6

Haddon stays with the horses in the dark alley behind the First Bank of Birthright. He is trying to keep them still and calm, but they know that there is violence in the air around them. The back door to the bank is ajar and Haddon has a clear view of the movement inside. What he can't see, his mind fills in at the sounds.

Calamine is standing above the bank manager, gun cocked, the barrel less than six inches from the back of the man's head. The manager is kneeling in front of the bank's only safe, stuffing the contents of it into a bloodstained pillowcase from his own bed. "Please," he says as he turns and hands the heavy bag to Calamine, "mister, please... I don't care who you are... please..."

Calamine stares at him as if he didn't hear a thing. "Take off your nightshirt," he says.

"What?" says the manager.

"Your nightshirt. Take it off." He does, and Calamine takes it from him and wraps it several times around the cylinder of his revolver. "See, this here," he says, "is where most of the sound comes out." He points the barrel at the center of the man's chest and fires. The sound is, indeed, muffled a little, but a gunshot still sounds like a gunshot, and the thump of a body hitting the floor still sounds the same, too. The bank manager's eyes are wide but unmoving, his mouth working up and down like a fish on the riverbank. His chest is a ruin of bone and blood, and the rhythmic pumping of what used to be his heart slows, then stops altogether.

Haddon is rooted to his place as Calamine walks with purpose out of the building, the bulging pillowcase in his fist. He ties it to the horn of Haddon's saddle, then moves to his own horse. He looks at Haddon, gives him a grin and a wink. Haddon shakes his head to try and come back to some sense of reality. Both men mount their horses at the same time and spur them into a gallop toward the dark edge of town.

No one comes running. No one gives chase. No one has heard a thing.

* * *

They ride hard for a while, then slower as the adrenaline subsides and they realize no one is following. Haddon isn't used to riding just by available starlight, and he stays tense, afraid that the horse will step into a hidden hole in the road and break its ankle, maybe injuring the rider in the fall. About the same time he thinks this, Calamine reins his horse in.

"Whoa, now..." Calamine looks around. "I think we best stop here for the night, Haddon. We need to get some sleep so that, in case we are discovered, we can ride hard again in the morning with light to see by and to see behind us." With that, he dismounts and leads his horse to a tangle of trees some two hundred feet from the road.

After a little while, a small but lively camp-fire burns before them. Haddon stares into the flames, seeing his past and trying to discern his future, but try as he might, he can't see one. It seems to end right there in the fire. Calamine is the first to break the stillness of the night. "Good to be free, ain't it?" he says.

Haddon's mind is still as knotted up as his conscience. "How do you mean?" he says.

"Just that," says Calamine. "Here we are. Free. Beholden to no one. Enough money to live without workin' for a while. Nobody to tell you that you ain't good enough. Free."

Haddon shakes his head. "I suppose," he says.

"Well," says Calamine, "you suppose correctly. Isn't this what you wanted, Haddon? To be somebody new? Somebody that people respected?"

"But at what price?"

"Don't matter, does it. No price is too high for self respect and a good reputation."

A dry laugh barks from Haddon's throat. "A good reputation? Is that what you think I have now? Because of you, my brother is dead, and people think I killed him! Because of you, a banker and his wife are dead—"

"Hold on there," says Calamine. "I don't think she's dead."

Haddon jumps to his feet and bends over toward Calamine. "Well, I beg your pardon. A banker is dead, and his wife *might* be, and there is no way that I won't be caught up in what you've done! I'm the one who was stupid enough to ride out with you, and somebody will come after us, it's only a matter of time. Yes sir, that's some reputation I have now, thank you very much!"

The dancing fire reflects off Calamine's grin. "You're welcome," he says.

Haddon sits back down in defeat. "I was employing the fine art of sarcasm."

Calamine's grin widens. "So was I."

Haddon sighs, then stirs the fire with a stick. A piece of wood collapses onto another under it and a shower of sparks spits out. Calamine watches them ascend. He speaks quietly into the night. "'Yet a man is born unto trouble, as surely as the sparks fly upward.' Job 5:7."

Haddon is only agitated by the quote. "That's another thing," says Haddon, "how do you know so much Scripture?"

"Well," says Calamine, "I've been around it a lot. If you don't mind me saying, I venture that I know about as much Scripture as you do. I can't preach it like you, though. You sure can do that."

Haddon throws the rest of the stick into the fire. It feels as useless in his hands as he feels in his heart. "Lot of good that did me," he says. "Just one more arrow of rejection in my back."

Calamine looks at him with something that could either be sympathy or contempt. "Don't you worry about those people, Haddon. They wouldn't know the gospel truth if it slapped them in the face. If they want to live their puny, helpless little lives lying to themselves and each other, let 'em. They didn't deserve you."

A grin slides onto Haddon's face for the first time in memory. "No," he says, "they didn't."

"And," continues Calamine, "if God is really who you say He is, He probably don't like those folks much, either."

Haddon scoots in toward Calamine a little and leans forward, anxious. "Well, that right there is part of the problem. If God is really who I have preached Him to be, then the fact is, He still loves them just as much as He does anybody. To be honest, that kind of sticks in my craw. How is that fair? For me to be honest and faithful and truthful, and for them to be two-faced, lying snakes, and yet He loves them the same as me? I don't know. Don't seem right, sometimes."

"And that," says Calamine," is why you have me. I balance the scales. Everybody needs one good friend they can count on, no matter what, who is always on their side. And I, sir, am that friend." Calamine leans back against a fallen log, takes out his gun and a pocket knife, and begins to scratch into the barrel of the revolver.

"What's that?" says Haddon.

"Come again?" says Calamine.

Haddon points to the knife. "What you're doing, right there. What is that?"

Calamine looks at his gun as if he didn't even know he was doing anything. Then, admiring his handiwork, he smiles. "Oh, this. Look here," he says, and he leans in toward Haddon and the firelight so that Haddon can see better. "I've had this gun since I was a boy. Remember? It's the gun I used when I taught you how to shoot."

A mist blows off of Haddon's mind for a moment, and in the clearing, he sees himself as a boy, with a young Calamine at his side, showing him how to load, aim, and fire his gun. The memory brings another smile.

"You know," says Haddon, "I had forgotten about that. You did teach me, didn't you?"

"Yessir," says Calamine, "and I taught you good, too, If I do say so myself. At least, after you got strong enough to hold the gun. You couldn't even do that when I first saw you."

Haddon's mind goes back a little bit further than before. "I remember that, too. The day my mama . . ."

A brief but lingering silence lowers itself between the men until Calamine speaks, shooing it away. "Yeah, well anyway, I liked this gun so much that I decided to brand it so's me and everybody would always know it's mine. So I started scratching my name in the barrel. See here?" Calamine uses the tip of the knife to point out the roughly engraved letters in the barrel of the gun. "Lookit—C-A-L-A and so forth. I keep going over it all the time, making it deeper and deeper." He laughs a little. "I guess when I can see the inside of the barrel, I'll stop." He leans back in to the log and continues, the faint metal on metal sound floating up in to the night like the sparks did earlier.

Haddon starts to say something, then stops. "Listen, . . ."

Calamine waits. "What?"

Haddon starts to try again, then waves the thought away. "No, never mind."

Calamine leans up again, his interest aroused. "No, go ahead, out with it."

"I've just been wanting to ask you," he says, "about your name. I never did know. Where did you get the name 'Calamine'?"

Calamine smiles. "Oh, that. It's more of a nickname, really. You see, some folks have an itchy trigger finger. Me? I'm just itchy all over, all the way through and through. See, Calamine is supposed to stop things from being itchy. That's why it's funny."

"Oh," says Haddon. "Well. At least I can stop wondering."

"I can tell you something else, Reverend," says Calamine. Haddon looks at him and feels his gaze, his dark eyes like deep pools of dangerous water. "You can stop wondering about a lot of things. Don't you worry about the future, Haddon. I will make sure that you get everything that you deserve, and God help anybody who wants to stop you from gettin' it." Calamine smiles again, and Haddon feels like a spell is broken. Calamine leans back against the log, sighs, and lowers his hat down over his face. "No sir, Mr. Haddon Chambers. 'Be not anxious for the morrow: for the morrow will be anxious for itself. Sufficient unto the day is the evil thereof.' Matthew 6:34. Yes, sir. 'Sufficient unto the day is the evil thereof.'"

The morning hours in Birthright, Texas are alive with the low hum of murmured rumors and fear. Sheriff Eli Blaylock stands staring at the pool of blood in front of the bank's steel safe. He isn't ready for this. Birthright is a quiet town, and he was assured that if he accepted the title of Sheriff, he wouldn't have to worry about this kind of thing. He doesn't even have a deputy. Now his friend Edgar is dead, lying over at the undertaker's, getting measured for his coffin. No word yet on whether Margaret will live or die. Eli is still staring at the blood, trying to corral his thoughts to figure out what to do next, when Bill, the saloon owner, shuffles respectfully up beside him.

"Mess, ain't it?" says Bill.

"I don't know what to think about this, Bill. I mean, ain't nobody in this town that would do something like this, is it? I mean, sometimes you never know about people, but Jesus, just look at this."

"And to think that Edgar was just sitting at my bar yesterday."

Something connects in Eli's mind. "Hey," he says, "Didn't you say we had a stranger in town yesterday?"

"Yeah," says Bill. "Wasn't here for long, but stopped in for a beer. Made a little bit of a ruckus, but I remember him."

Edgar considers this. "Who do we got around here that can draw, Bill?"

"Well, I seen some things that Millie Fields, Dan's daughter, has done. She's a pretty good little artist."

"Would you go visit the Fields and see if she can draw a picture based on your description? I'm gonna have to contact the Rangers' office about this, and it would be good to have something to give them."

"Sure," says Bill, "I'll go over right now."

"I appreciate it. Bring it over when you get it, would you? I'm gonna go send a telegram and see if we can get some help here." Eli's gaze follows the trail of bloody footprints that lead out the back door to the alley. "I think we're gonna need a tracker."

CHAPTER 7

Haddon is tired of moving and sore from riding when they reach the Trinity River outside of Fort Worth. At a fairly secluded bend in the river, Haddon takes as thorough a bath as he can without soap, before he goes into the city to make his next move. He knows he can't get himself as presentable as he would like, but at least he can rinse off the dust and sweat of nearly four days of travel.

He dries in the sun, beats as much of the dust from his clothes as possible, and dresses again.

Haddon makes it a point to swing wide of the area known as Hell's Half Acre. He has trouble aplenty without running into the kinds of people who reportedly inhabit those lawless blocks. Calamine is bad company enough.

After another half hour, Haddon and Cal-amine ride slowly under a sign that stretches across the street, a sign that says *Fort Worth Stockyards*. It is a growing city, trying to set itself apart from Dallas to the east, and trying even harder to attract a better class of people than the cattle drovers and outlaws that are drawn to the seedy side of town. Haddon takes it in. He has made a decision, and it's time to come out with it. He looks straight ahead when he speaks.

"We need to part ways here," he says. Cala-mine looks at Haddon for a long minute. Had-don continues. "I know that you think I need you to protect me," he says, "but I don't. This is where I make a new start, all on my own. I know that it was you who has gotten me this far, for good or for evil, but here we are. I do appreciate your loyalty and your . . . help . . . but I must make my own stand now." Finally, he turns to-ward Calamine. "Do you understand that?"

Calamine thinks for a minute, then smiles and looks down. "Of course I understand," he says. "In fact, I think I understand even more than you do, at least about some things. See, what I also understand is that, even though you have found your sand, there will come a time, probably sooner rather than later, when you will need me again."

Haddon starts to protest, but Calamine holds up a hand and says, "It's okay, don't worry, I ain't arguing with you. I'm just telling you now so that you can remember it later. When you need me—and you will—I'll know it. Until then, you won't even know I'm around, but you can go to sleep knowing that I will be. Around. Close by. Now, whether that is cause for comfort or concern . . . well, I guess that's up to you." Calamine tips his hat toward Haddon. "Good day, Mr. Chambers," he says. "And good luck to you." With that, Calamine tugs on his horse's reins, the horse trots off to the left, and Calamine disappears in the shadows between two buildings on Main Street.

Haddon rides a few more blocks before dismounting and tying his horse to a hitching post in front of a deceptively unimpressive building. Haddon knows that just behind the big plate glass windows are the offices of the *Fort Worth Daily Gazette*, the largest newspaper in Tarrant County. Haddon removes his hat, straightens his posture, turns the knob, and enters.

His entrance goes largely unnoticed, the sound of the door being drowned out by the hum and clacking of the constantly moving press machinery that fills the large space. Haddon approaches what looks to be a receptionist's desk. A stern-looking but not unattractive woman is reading a paper and doesn't look up at him.

"Excuse me . . ." says Haddon.

She still doesn't look at him.

"Yes sir?" she says.

"I wondered if I could see Mr. Paddock?"

"Who are you looking for?"

"Mr. Buckley Paddock. The editor of this paper. Is he in?"

Finally, her eyes swivel upward enough to take him in. "Oh," she says. "No, he's not in."

"Well then," Haddon presses, " Is there an assistant editor who is in?"

The woman gives up trying to ignore him completely. "What do you need, sir?" she says.

"Well," says Haddon, "I'm a writer. A reporter. I just got into town and wanted to introduce myself."

"Oh, alright," says the woman. "Just a minute." She makes sure Haddon hears a loud sigh as she rises from her chair and walks around behind her desk into a windowed office, where she speaks with a slightly older man, balding, a bit overweight with a pipe clenched between his teeth. Haddon can't hear what the woman is saying, but she is clearly not happy about being interrupted. The man listens for a moment, then responds with a look somewhere between irritation and exasperation as he waves her back to her post. He rubs his eyes, looks through the window at Haddon, and waves him in.

As Haddon walks into the office, the man rises from behind his desk and extends his hand. "Lyman Easton. How can I help you son?" he says.

Haddon shakes his hand and says, "Mr. Easton, I am here to offer my services as a writer in any capacity that you need me."

"Well, we aren't hiring right now, but check back with us in a month or two."

"Oh," says Haddon, "I'm not looking to be paid, Mr. Easton, at least not right away. I have enough money to last me a little while, so I thought I would write for you on a trial basis, so to speak, until you see that you just can't go on without me."

Lyman is genuinely surprised. "Is that a fact?"

"Yessir, that's a fact."

"Well," says Lyman, "who am I to turn down free work? You any good?"

"I believe I am," says Haddon. I am well read and I can spell better than anyone you have working on this paper. I can put words together that will make the monthly meeting of the Flower Arrangement Society sound like the convening of the House of Representatives. All I ask is a chance to prove it."

Lyman Easton considers for a moment, while he tries to discern if this boy actually might be worth his spit. He offers his hand again in agreement. "Chance given," he says. "What's your name, son?"

Haddon beams and returns the handshake. "Haddon Chambers, sir. Wesley Haddon Chambers."

The names remind Lyman of something, then he smiles. "Your mama must have wanted you to be a preacher."

A darkness passes over Haddon's mind like a restless ghost. "Well," he says, "that is neither here nor there as concerns my writing, is it?"

Lyman puts his hands up in defense and chuckles. "Hey," he says, "No worry, no worry, just an observation, that's all."

Haddon's face lightens again. "When may I start?"

Lyman looks around the office. Well, seeing how I don't have to pay you, I'd say you just did. Find a horizontal surface anywhere around here to call your own, as long as there is nobody else already at it, and bring me a story when you have one."

"I will, sir," says Haddon. "And thank you. You won't regret it."

Lyman puts on a playful frown. "See that I don't," he says, then winks.

Haddon leaves that office a different man from the one who came in. For the first time in a long time, he feels a wind blowing from a different direction, and it carries the scent of good changes. *This is it*, he thinks. *A new start. A new life. This is it.*

* * *

The afternoon sun in Birthright, Texas makes the air in Sheriff Eli's office as oppressive as the mood of the town. Eli is behind his desk, and in front sits a tall man with leathery skin and a large gray moustache that covers most of his mouth. He has folded his lanky frame onto a small ladderback chair, but he doesn't convey any discomfort to the Sheriff. It's as if he has sat lots of different places in his life, and one suits him as well as another. The two men have been talking for some time, even though there isn't a lot to say.

"Yessir," says Eli, "that's about the sum total of it, Ranger."

The tall man waves off the formality. "You can call me Tyson," he says.

"If it ain't too forward for you," says Eli.

"Titles don't make authority, Sheriff. Tyson is fine."

"Then you can make it even and call me Eli."

Ranger Montgomery Tyson gets back to business. "So," he says, "he just rode in, kidnapped the bank manager, pistol whipped his wife, robbed the bank, then murdered the bank manager, and rode out of town? All in the course of a day?"

"That's the size of it," says Eli. "No hotel room, no purchase at the store. Only reason you have that drawing in your hands is because he bought a drink down to the saloon. At least we think so. Only stranger anybody remembers from that day, but don't necessarily mean it was him."

"Part of a gang?" asks the Ranger.

Eli shrugs. "No way to know. Could be. Could have had somebody hiding just out of town for the robbery or the getaway or both."

Tyson thinks, and shakes his head. "Anything else at all?"

"Well," says Eli, "I guess there is one other thing."

To Tyson's mind, anything new is important. "Yes? What is it?"

"Well, when he was in the saloon, somebody heard him yellin' the words 'Black Ankle.'"

"That's it?" says Tyson. "Black Ankle?"

"Yes sir. If I'm not badly mistaken, I believe it's a town a couple of days' ride east of here."

Tyson rubs his chin, and the stubble makes a soft scratching sound in the room. "Not much to go on, is it?" he says.

"No sir, I'm afraid not. Wish I could do more for you. Edgar—the banker—was a good man. A friend."

Tyson nods with sympathy. "How's his wife?"

"Don't know yet," says Eli. "Still unconscious. Calls for him every now and again, though. Sad, sad thing. I hope you catch this fella, or them fellas—whichever it may be."

Tyson puts his hat on and stands to his full height. "Oh, that I will do, Eli. That I will do." He walks to the door and turns around. "You folks have a Western Union office in town?"

CHAPTER 8

The streets and sidewalks outside the offices of the *Fort Worth Gazette* are still bustling with activity, except that now it's less about a day's work as it is a night's unwinding. Some are headed to the nearest saloon, while others are headed to their home and family. Lyman Easton is one of the latter kind.

Lyman pushes back a belly length from his desk, stands and puts on his coat while he looks around the newsroom. In a corner, he sees Haddon with a stack of back issues, poring over them and making notes on a separate sheet of paper. He walks over and speaks to him gently, so as not to startle him. "Time to call it a day, young man," he says.

Haddon looks up at him, tearing his attention from the papers. "Oh, that's fine, yes. Sorry.

I was trying to familiarize myself with the kind of stories that the paper reports."

"Is that right?" says Lyman. "You want to make sure that whatever you bring in fits?"

Haddon stands and reaches for his hat. "No, not exactly. I want to make sure that what I write stands out from the rest."

Lyman is surprised, but the perspective pleases him. "I see," he says. "Well, that just makes good sense, now, doesn't it? At any rate, there is plenty of time for that later. Where are you staying?"

"Nowhere, as of yet," says Haddon. "I came here first thing after arriving in town. I figured I would find a hotel for the next couple of days, then maybe a good boarding house for a while after that."

There is something about this boy that Lyman is drawn to, he just can't put his finger on it yet. But something. "Well," he says, "I can't speak for my wife past supper tonight, but why don't you come home with me and join us for a meal, then we'll see where to go from there."

"Well," says Haddon, "alright, that sounds fine, thank you. If it isn't too much trouble."

Lyman waves off the thanks. "No trouble 't all, young man, no trouble 't all. My carriage is out back. Bring your horse on around and you can follow me."

Riding west, back across the Trinity River, the sun is beginning its descent in front of them. Haddon watches with admiration as it paints the sky with colors that he has either never seen, or maybe not allowed himself to actually look at. The expanse of sky facing him is very different from the pine-crowded woods of home. *Home.* Haddon isn't even sure what the word means anymore, until he and Lyman round a bend in the road and approach a modest but spacious house on a few acres. As they draw closer, the house gives off a soft glow from inside, almost like the windows are smiling at him.

Haddon ties his horse to a top fence rail beside the house as Lyman slides out of the carriage, letting gravity help him to the ground. They stand in the yard for a moment, and Lyman looks up at the young man. "Well," he says, "she ain't much to look at, but she sure knows how to welcome you home."

"Oh," says Haddon, "I think it's a fine house."

Lyman's eyebrows go up. "That it is," he says, "but I was talking about my wife!" Then he laughs, and Haddon thinks that maybe he has never really heard anyone laugh before. There is a timbre in it that feels like it has been dropped into his soul like a seed. It's like something in him is being gently shaken awake.

Lyman and Haddon mount the few steps and scrape their boots on a floor-mounted brush beside the front door. Lyman opens the door and they enter, hanging their hats and coats on a rack. Inside, the light from the setting sun has somehow taken up residence in the house. The air is yellow and warm, and it smells like contentment.

"Come on in, son," says Lyman. "I can tell by the aroma that my Ada has been busy. It is biscuit day in the Easton home." Lyman turns toward the open doorway to the kitchen. "Ada!" he calls.

From the kitchen, another voice calls back. "Yes, dear!" says Ada.

"I have but one question for you!" Lyman says.

Ada appears in the doorway, wiping her hands on a flour-dusted apron. She isn't round, but not thin, either, thinks Haddon. She looks—well—pleasant. Her sandy blonde hair is pulled up into a bun, but some strands are straggling down by her face, which is still a little florid from the heat of the kitchen and the labor of supper. "What might that be, husband?" she says.

Lyman takes one step toward her and stops. "It is simply this: How do I love thee?"

"Hmmm," says Ada, taking one step toward

Lyman and stopping, too. "Let me count the ways."

Lyman takes another step. "I love thee to the depth and breadth and height my soul can reach, when feeling out of sight. For the ends of Being and Ideal Grace..."

Another step and the next line from Ada: "I love thee to the level of every day's most quiet need, by sun and candlelight..."

Lyman, another step. "I love thee fiercely, as men strive for Right..."

Ada, closer again. "I love thee purely, as they turn from Praise..."

Haddon looks on, transfixed. Lyman steps again. "I love thee with a passion put to use in my old griefs, and with my childhood's faith..."

They are now within reach of each other, and each take the other's hands while never breaking their gaze. Ada, again: "I love thee with a love I seemed to lose with my lost saints..."

Lyman smiles at her. "I love thee with the breath..."

"Smiles..."

"Tears..."

"Of all my life. And, if God so choose..."

Lyman speaks more softly than before. "I shall love thee better after death." Lyman and Ada share a kiss, small, but full of meaning and history. Haddon is still watching the whole exchange like an explorer who is hearing an unknown language for the first time.

"Hello, my dear," says Lyman.

"Welcome home. Supper is almost ready." Ada nods toward Haddon. "And who is this young man?"

Haddon steps forward a little. "My name is Haddon Chambers, ma'am."

Lyman says, "He is new to our fair city, just rode in and offered his services to the newspaper. He has nowhere to stay just yet, so I invited him to our home for supper." Then, whispering aside to Haddon with full intention of Ada's hearing, he pats his stomach and says, "She always makes too much food, anyway."

Ada rises to the challenge. "Well," she says, "if you like, I can just quit cooking for you altogether. Then you might lose some weight."

"Hold on, now," says Lyman, "there is no call for that kind of talk. I'll have Haddon here write an article about how you are threatening to murder me by starvation!"

Ada turns and heads back to the kitchen. "Well," she says over her shoulder, "I'm quite sure that he won't find any evidence of you starving after seeing you at the table tonight." She turns and addresses Haddon again before entering the kitchen. "Haddon, we are having pork chops, mustard greens, biscuits, and tomato gravy. I hope that's agreeable with you?"

"Oh, yes, ma'am," says Haddon. "I honestly can't remember the last time I had a meal like that."

"Good. The only price you will have to pay is to set out some plates—they are on the sideboard, there—and, the worst penalty, of all, you will have to listen to the god-awful noises that my husband makes as he drowns himself in gravy."

Ada disappears from the doorway, and Lyman looks at Haddon and shrugs. "Gravy is my favorite beverage," he says.

* * *

Texas Ranger Montgomery Tyson sits on the edge of a borrowed bed in a borrowed room above the saloon in Birthright. He slips his boots off and flexes his feet and toes inside of worn red socks. The heat of the day has lessened, but the humidity has hung on. Tyson can't help but keep puzzling over where the next step in this investigation might lead. Maybe he will get an answer soon from his counterpart over in east Texas.

A soft knock on the door sharpens his senses. Soft doesn't always mean safe. Tyson slips his Walker Colt out of its holster on the bedpost and holds it easily by his leg, resting it on the bed. "Come in," he says.

A young man pushes the door partway open but remains in the hallway. Tyson recognizes him as the saloon owner's middle son, who also acts as a bellhop for tips. "Ranger Tyson?" he says. "I have a telegram for you, sir. Sheriff Eli said I should wait for it at the telegraph office, seein's how you was waitin' for it, and that I should run it on over to you."

Tyson relaxes, but holds on to the gun. "That's fine," he says, "thank you. Bring it on over."

The bellhop steps into the room and hands the telegraph to Tyson. Tyson begins to read it, then realizes after a moment that the boy is still standing there, watching him, his right hand stretched out, palm up. Tyson digs into his vest pocket and tosses a couple of coins into the boy's hand. "Thank you, sir," the boy says. "You have a good night, sir."

Tyson nods as the boy backs out and shuts the door behind him. He looks down at the paper again and reads it:

HEARD FROM FRIEND IN BLACK ANKLE. COULD BE SAME. LIT OUT MORNING AFTER MURDER. DESCRIPTION FITS.

Tyson lays the telegram on the small table beside the bed and sighs. He slides the gun back into its holster and swings his long legs up and onto the bed. His legs hang off the end of the bed from mid-calf down. Just like always in a bed not his own. He stares up at the ceiling and thinks.

* * *

Supper has been successfully eaten at the Easton home, the last drop of tomato gravy has been sopped up by the last biscuit, and it disappears down the grateful throat of Haddon Chambers. Ada has been watching him with a smile. "I would ask if you enjoyed that, Haddon," she says, " but I don't think I've seen you take a breath since your first bite!"

Haddon comes up for that breath now and is reminded of where he is. "Yes, ma'am," he says, "it was delicious. I hope you are not offended by the ardor with which I have supped."

Ada laughs and fans herself with her fan. "Well, I do declay-ah!" she says. "We have an educated man among us, Mr. Easton!"

Lyman nods and finishes his iced tea. "I would hope so. Otherwise he won't be worth spit as a reporter."

A small silence settles on the table as Haddon makes a decision to broach a subject. "May I ask you both a question?" he says.

Ada answers first, while beginning to stack dishes on each other for carrying to the kitchen. "Of course, son," she says.

"When we came in," says Haddon. "The sonnet..."

Lyman chuckles, and a burp escapes with it. "I thought you might ask about that eventually," he says. He turns to Ada. "May I explain, dearest?"

Ada pushes back from the table and picks up a stack of plates. "Be my guest, Mr. Easton." As she stands and carries two full hands of the residue of supper into the kitchen, Lyman takes a moment to gather his thoughts, then says, "I memorized that particular Elizabeth Barrett Browning sonnet when I was courting Mrs. Easton, in order to impress her, and impress her it did. Then she learned it and recited it to me at our wedding." Haddon watches as a cloud passes over Lyman's face. Not a dark cloud, but a shadow of one. Lyman motions him up from the table. "Come," he says, "sit with me."

Lyman leads Haddon across the room to where two wingback chairs and a sofa are arranged around a flagstone fireplace, with small tables scattered around for ease of use. Lyman sits in one of the chairs and motions for Haddon to take the other one. Lyman lifts a brown, rusticated briar pipe out of a stand on the table next to his chair, and pulls a pouch of tobacco from a jar next to the stand.

Haddon watches and waits as Lyman fills the pipe, tamps the tobacco down, then fills it again. He strikes a match and lets it hover over the flame, then inhales into the pipe and draws the flame down onto the tobacco, where it burns red and curls for a moment. A curl of cherry scented blue smoke streams up and billows away. And before the match goes out, Haddon sees it reflected in the tears in Lyman's eyes.

"We had a son, Haddon," Lyman says. "Wonderful boy. Smart, like you. Would be about your age now. His name was Lucas. He was the joy of our hearts. One day, Lucas was swimming with friends in the Trinity River, when he just went under one time and didn't come back up. Simple as that. No other reason. Here, then gone."

"I—I'm sorry," says Haddon. "I didn't mean to open old wounds."

Lyman shakes his head and smiles through the tears. "Oh, no apologies. That's a good word for it, though, an old wound. He was twelve or so, some dozen years ago now. Anyhow, Mrs. Easton and I could tell that afterwards, we were drowning, too, in our grief. Both of us sad, every day, all day. A couple of months later, we decided to pull each other out of the waves. We promised to give each other that sonnet—<u>our</u> sonnet—every day for the rest of our lives." He takes another draw of his pipe, tamps down the coals, and lights it again. Another exhale of blue smoke. "And do you know what, son?" he says. "That sonnet saved our lives. We began to breathe again, as we held each other close with those words. And, in time, we were able to talk about Lucas and smile instead of weeping. Oh, the hurt is always there. But love, my boy, is stronger than hurt. Always has been. Always will be." He inhaled again, let the smoke escape his lips, and settled back into the chair. He looks over his shoulder and hears Ada still clearing the table. Then he says, a bit louder than his tone up to now, "And the first day that old lady doesn't hear that sonnet from me, young Haddon, well, that will be the day that I have decided I am done with her and ready to move on to the next young filly. Ask me, that day is coming, and none too soon, either."

Ada doesn't even bother to turn around as she heads back into the kitchen with more dishes. "Which will also be the day," she says, "that someone comes to her senses and poisons your gravy. Not saying who, but someone."

A while later, Haddon stands in a bedroom in the Easton home and looks around. It is homey in a way that he has never seen. Warm. Inviting. Quilts are draped over a chair, as well as stacked in a corner. A bookcase is home to all kinds of books: *Huck Finn, Oliver Twist, The Strange Case of Dr. Jekyll and Mr. Hyde, a Webster's Dictionary*. The door swings open behind him, and Ada enters, bearing towels and soap. "Thank you again," says Haddon, "for the room tonight. You didn't have to do that. I have money for a hotel."

"Nonsense," says Ada. "Besides, knowing Lyman like I do, you will need to save your money. There will be snow on the sun before he decides to pay you for writing." She lays the soap and towels on the bed, with a few other items. "So," she says, "here is a towel, soap, and a toothbrush. I didn't know what you might have with you."

"None of those things," says Haddon. "Thank you." Haddon looks around the room and notices a crude but lovingly drawn map, framed on the wall above the bed. It shows the Easton home, and a long, squiggly line that leads to Mineral Wells, Texas. There is another house drawn there, above another wavy line that says *Brazos*. Haddon nods toward it. "May I ask what this map shows?"

Ada walks over to it, reaches out, touches it lightly, and smiles. "Our Lucas drew that himself. Lyman has a fishing cabin on a bluff overlooking the Brazos River. It's short for 'Brazos De Dios'—'the arms of God'. Lucas loved that place, and the trips he took there with his father. This map is actually very accurate."

Haddon is captured by it. He imagines being there, himself. In his mind, he walks those roads and fishes in that river. "It sounds beautiful," he says.

Ada is seeing the details, too. "It is," she says. "In fact, we buried Lucas there. He loved it so much. *In the arms of God*." As if a pleasant spell is broken, she looks away from the map and turns to Haddon. "Well—is there anything you need?"

"No, ma'am," says Haddon, "I don't think so. Thank you again for taking me in."

"It is our pleasure. As you might have guessed, this was Lucas' room, but we are not the sort of people to have kept everything the way it was, like a shrine. I'm not faulting those folks, but we needed to move on, to keep healing. Still, it's good to see someone in here again. You sure there's nothing else you need?"

"No, ma'am, I don't believe there is," says Haddon.

Ada pats him on the arm and moves toward the door. "Well, good night, then, Haddon, " she says. "Sleep well."

After she leaves the room, Haddon sits on the edge of the bed and looks around, taking it all in. He turns and looks at the map again, for a long time. With a satisfied smile, he lies down on the bed and closes his eyes. As he drifts off to sleep, he tries to leave the past few days behind him. As his breathing settles, he isn't even in a bed anymore. He is dozing on the banks of the Brazos, cane pole in his hands, a bobber dipping in the ripples of the cool water.

CHAPTER 9

Birthright, Texas
Birthright Hotel and Saloon

Sheriff Eli stands on the porch of the Birthright hotel and watches as Ranger Tyson cinches up his saddle. The morning air is bright and crisp, and the town has not yet begun to stir among the storefronts. "Where will you go from here, Tyson?" he asks.

"Well," says Tyson, "I suppose I need to start at the beginning, which appears to be Black Ankle. There's an old blind man in those parts who seems to know something about everything that happens around there. I'll stop along the way and show around the drawing, ask if anybody has seen anyone like my man. If I find answers, I'll head back west and start tracking from here again. I'll just keep moving and stopping until I get a lead."

"Do keep me informed, if you would," says Eli. "I'd like to have something to say to the people of my town as they ask me."

Tyson straightens his saddle blanket and takes hold of the horn. "I'll do that. I will also let you and my friends at the Rangers office know where I am from time to time, in case any more information comes to light."

"I appreciate it, Ranger, I sure do." Tyson mounts his horse and looks down at Eli from the height. Eli runs a hand through his thinning hair and nods toward his fellow lawman. "Good luck to you, Ranger Montgomery Tyson," he says.

Tyson tips his hat. "Thank you, Sheriff. You'll be hearing from me." He gives a short, high whistle, and the horse turns on his command and heads toward the edge of town. Tyson spurs it into a gallop and sets his eyes like flint toward Black Ankle.

*　　*　　*

Haddon feels as if he has awakened into someone else's life. The bedroom is cool and pleasant, a fragrant spring breeze blowing in the window past billowing curtains. He slides out of the bed and walks over to the partially open window and raises it higher. An idyllic backyard lies before him, a chicken coop and small animal pen, followed by a green field and a fishing pond behind it. He hears the wings of ducks beating against the surface of the pond, and he can't tell if they are playing, fighting, or just bathing. Maybe in this new life he can learn those kinds of things.

Haddon gets dressed and follows the smell of bacon and eggs into the dining room, where Lyman is just sitting down. "Good morning, Mr. and Mrs. Easton," he says.

"Well, there," says Lyman, "Good morning, Haddon. I figured the smell would draw you out but I was coming to get you for breakfast if it had not done so."

"It certainly smells delicious," says Haddon, "but shouldn't we be getting to the paper soon?"

Lyman is confused for a moment, then it dawns on him. "The paper?" he says. You must have been traveling hard, son. It's Saturday. I don't go to work on Saturday, and neither will you, not even for free. Come, sit."

Haddon is happy to take a seat in front of steaming bowls of scrambled eggs, grits, sausage gravy, fresh biscuits, and homemade blackberry jam. Mrs. Easton walks up and places a plate of sizzling bacon on the table as she takes her seat on the other side. Lyman takes her hand and holds his other hand out for Haddon's. Haddon takes his hand and the Eastons bow their heads.

"Dear Lord," Lyman prays, "we are grateful to thee for all of thy bountiful blessings in our lives. We thank thee for letting us have Lucas for a season, and we know that he is well with you. We thank thee today for our new friend Haddon, and we pray thou wilt pour out untold blessing upon him in everything that he seeks. Now, please bless this food to the nourishment of our bodies, and our bodies to thy service. Amen."

"Amen," echoes Ada.

"Amen," a moment later from Haddon.

Ada unfolds a napkin onto her lap and reaches for a biscuit and the jam. "Well, Haddon," she says, "tell us about yourself. Where are you from?"

Before Haddon can answer, Lyman puts up a hand. "Hold on a minute, Ada, that may be a subject that young Haddon here may not be comfortable discussing with people he just met."

"Then he is welcome to decline to answer, dear," says Ada. "I believe a smart young man like this is able to answer for himself, don't you?"

Lyman nods in concession. "The point is yours, my dear."

Ada says, "Please don't feel obligated, Haddon. I am just a curious sort about other people's stories. But not to the point of gossip, mind you. The Bible is very clear about gossiping and busybodying. I shall leave that to the newspaper."

Lyman mimes an arrow going into his heart, but chuckles at the barb. The question has almost involuntarily taken Haddon back to where he doesn't want to be. He feels a shadow rise up inside of him as he speaks. "I come from a nowhere town of nobody people," he says. "It's a few days' ride east of here. It is a dark, lonely piece of dirt, where you can't take a breath without someone being disappointed in you, and the pine tress hover over you like they have been appointed by God to keep you from seeing the sky or looking for a way out."

Lyman and Ada have stopped eating. They are stunned by the gravity of the moment before Lyman dabs his mouth with a napkin and finds his voice again. "Well," he says, "I can see that the paper is certainly going to acquire some much needed eloquence in its pages."

Ada reaches a hand gently across the table and lays it on top of Haddon's clenched fist. "I am sorry, Haddon. I truly am. Sorry for whatever kind of life has left such a dark stain on your soul. It is obvious that you are a man of profound depth and perception, and I am sorry for you that it has not been nurtured and watered."

Haddon is still haunted by the memories, but he is feeling a little more vulnerable here, in this place. Like he can say anything. "Stomped on and scoffed at is closer to it," he says. "Suffocated, really." He takes a breath and wonders if he should go further. He decides he will. "My mother died when I was young, but I also had an older brother. He's dead, too, and not long ago. My father. . . my father did not take it well."

"Son," says Lyman, "I don't know your father, and I hope you will forgive me for saying so, but there just ain't no way on God's green earth for a man to take that well."

Haddon looks at Lyman for a moment before he nods with understanding. "If it were anyone else who told me that, I would probably tell them off and walk away. But you have a right to say it, Mr. Easton, and so it does not offend me. There is even a part of me that knows you're right, but... well, he blames me."

"Now that, son," says Lyman, "I do not understand. Even in grief, a father must hold his tongue so as never to give a son a sense of shame and guilt, especially when he has nothing to be ashamed or guilty of. I am sure you had nothing to do with it."

Haddon shrugs and takes a deeper breath. "Well, be that as it may," he says, "I can never go back. My stepmother will most likely forgive and forget me over time. I know that sounds cruel, but I think it's true. She will move on to other things."

Ada looks at Lyman and he gives her a nod. "Haddon," she says, "Mr. Easton and I have discussed it some already thing morning, and we don't want you to be in a hurry to find a boarding house. You are welcome to stay with us here for as long as you need to. Of course, you will eventually want to be on your own, you're a young man building a new life, after all. But for now, please consider our home to be yours, if you like."

Haddon has never heard real kindness before now, and he's not sure he knows how to respond appropriately. He decides on a shy "Thank you."

Lyman claps his hands together and looks at Ada. "Dear," he says, "do you have any more questions that might probe like a hot needle into the very core of young Mr. Chambers' heart, or can I get you to pass me the grits?"

Midmorning, Haddon sits in one of the comfortable living room chairs reading the book by Robert Louis Stevenson that he found in his bedroom—*is it wrong to think of it as his, he wonders?*—when he hears a noise out in the front yard. He walks to the window and looks out. There, he sees Lyman trying unsuccessfully to load some logs onto a wagon. Like echoes from the back of a cold, dark cave, he hears his own voice—*I could have helped Daddy and Ethan out there...*

I know you think you could, comes the echo of Abigail. *But it's best not to chance it. You're just not as strong as your brother... you know that...you know that...*

Before he realizes what he is doing or why, he reaches for the knob of the front door and steps out onto the porch. "Mind if I help you, Mr. Easton? I know I don't look like much, but..."

Lyman mops his brow with a checkered bandana and smiles at him. "Don't matter much what you look like, son," he says. "What matters is what you are in your heart and what you are willing to learn. I don't know how it happens, but these danged logs get heavier every year, it seems. Just the way God designed it, I suppose. I would welcome your help, son."

Haddon goes down the steps with a spring in his walk that looks very unlike the Haddon

Chambers of Black Ankle. He bends down, takes one end of a log as Lyman takes the other, and together, they hoist it onto the wagon with a thump.

For the next several hours, Haddon works like a lion let out of a cage. The wood on the wagon is to repair a broken fence post, and only the briefest flash of Ethan at his last fencepost streaks across Haddon's mind. After that, Haddon climbs on the roof where some shingles have blown off. With some guidance from Lyman on the ground, Haddon navigates the roofline and nails down the new ones. The Eastons have one ornery cow, and she needs to be milked again, so Haddon gets to it, avoiding her flicking tail and flying hooves. By midafternoon, new chicken wire is strung around the chicken yard, as a fox looks on from the tree line, disappointed, then sulking away. And through it all, Haddon and Lyman talk, about anything and everything having to do with the state of the world and the newspaper's place in it.

The light of the day grows purple, unnoticed, and the bullfrogs start their chorus. Haddon and Lyman slowly climb the front steps, dirty and ragged and sweaty, but still chuckling at something one of them has said. They lower themselves into two rocking chairs on the porch and watch as the sunset shoots orange rays into the western Fort Worth sky from behind the trees. Haddon looks at the expanse, amazed. The tall pines of east Texas never gave him this kind of view. "You know, Mr. Easton," he says, "I can't imagine there could ever be enough clouds to fill up this sky at once."

Lyman fans himself with his hat. "You'd think that," he says, "but it happens, and sometimes when it does, you don't want to be caught out in it."

The front door creaks open and Ada emerges with a silver serving tray and two tall glasses of iced lemonade. She hands one to each of the men. Lyman says, "Thank you, my dear, this is fine, just fine." He turns and clinks his glass softly against Haddon's. "And thank you, Haddon, for all of your help today. That little set of chores would have taken me two months to do all by myself."

"And that," says Ada, "would have been after he decided to actually get started."

Lyman shakes his head and says, "I'm always telling her, Haddon, if a wife asks her husband to do something, let him do it. There's no sense nagging him about it every six months."

Ada brushes some dust off of the porch swing with a napkin, then sits in it and pushes back a little to get it going. "You certainly did work hard today, Haddon," she says, "and we are both grateful."

"Well," says Haddon, "I should be the one thanking you, honestly. I never got the chance to work like that back home. I wanted to, mind you, but—well, Daddy said I was weak and Abigail was afraid I would get sick again."

A mother's concern animates Ada's face. "You were sick as a child?"

"Yes, ma'am," says Haddon. "Not the whole time, but once, and very seriously. Yellow fever. I had it for weeks and almost died, they tell me. I was, in fact, very weak for a long time after."

"But not forever," says Ada.

"No, not forever. At least I didn't think so. I wanted to prove that I was strong like my brother but no one was listening. I was left to myself most of the time, so I read books. Studied them, more like it."

Lyman takes a sip of lemonade. "If you couldn't outwork him," he says, "maybe you could outsmart him?"

Haddon shrugs. "I suppose that's what it was. Not consciously, but it was the only way I knew to compete."

Lyman leans back in his chair and sets it to rocking. "See, that right there," he says, "is the problem. Forgive me if it sounds like I am speaking against your daddy, I mean I have never met the man. But I don't need to meet him to tell you that a father shouldn't ever make his children feel like they are in competition with each other. Now, I'm not saying that life isn't full of challenges and competition, it most certainly is. But every child should feel like they have all of their father's or mother's love, no matter how many children are under that roof." Lyman watches the sky for a moment, then smiles. "Of course, that's just me talking. I only got to practice with one, but I like to think that we—me and Mrs. Easton—gave him the best twelve years a boy could have. I like to think that Lucas never doubted how strongly he was loved. And that—that right there, loving my only boy with everything I had for his whole life—that is the one thing I will be proudest of when it comes time for me to let slip this mortal coil and walk through eternity's portal and bid this life goodbye." He takes another long sip of lemonade and looks at Haddon. "I don't know if that makes any sense to you, Haddon," he says, "but there it is. The meaning of life." The wink that he gives makes Haddon to know that even though he believes every word he just said, he still doesn't take himself all that seriously.

Haddon nods and says, "I think that makes more sense than anything I have ever heard." He pauses for a moment. "I just wish..." He shakes his head and looks down.

"What do you wish, dear?" asks Ada.

When Haddon opens his mouth, the words in his heart come tumbling out. "I wish I had been your son! I have felt more love from the two of you in the past twenty-four hours than I did in twenty-four years back home. It's hard to even call it 'home'. If you don't mind me saying it, I would have traded twenty-four years of the life I had, just for twelve years of living with you."

As those words sprawl out on the porch among them, Haddon is suddenly uncomfortable with the raw quality of the moment. "I'm sorry," he says as he stands and shuffles away a little. "You barely know me... I didn't mean to assert myself so... I usually don't say things like that."

Ada smiles, stands, and walks over to him like she is feeding a stray puppy that is scared and unsure. "You mean," she says, "that you have never said anything like that before."

Haddon stops moving away. "Yes ma'am," he says.

Ada takes his hands in hers and speaks, soft, but firm. "Then it's high time you started. And that, strong young man, was a very good start."

CHAPTER 10

Old Man Spragg's house
Just north of Black Ankle, Texas

Texas Ranger Montgomery Tyson sits on the edge of a small horsehair couch, facing an old blind man in a worn but comfortable looking wingback chair. Tyson figures that chair wouldn't hold anyone else if they tried to sit in, it's gotten so used to the old man's weight and shape. Old Man Spragg says, "How's the coffee, Ranger? You good?"

"Yessir, I'm fine, thank you," says Tyson. "So this young man, Haddon..."

"Chambers," says Spragg.

"Chambers, yessir. He just showed up all hot and bothered out of nowhere?"

"Well, not exactly out of nowhere," says Spragg. "Family lives on a hardscrabble farm down by the piney creek. He came on a day of trouble."

"Trouble?" says Tyson.

"Yessir, trouble indeed. Seems his big brother was shot in the head the night before."

Tyson looks down into the tin cup of coffee, as if the answers are there, about to float to the surface, but not visible yet. "Why did he come to see you?" he asks.

Spragg smiles. "Why did you come to see me, Ranger?"

"See if you had any answers for me."

Spragg nods at him. "There you have it, then. 'Ceptin' he wasn't looking for the same kind of answers you are." Spragg tilts his head as if he is looking into the corner. "I sure hope he has found them."

Tyson follows the only thread he has. "Mr. Spragg," he says, "did he seem like the kind of boy who would kill his brother?"

Spragg leans back into his chair. "Haddon Chambers? No sir, not at all. But Calamine did."

Tyson isn't sure he heard correctly. "Sorry?" he says. "Who?"

Spragg chuckles at remembering the odd name. "Calamine. That's who the boy told me about. Said Calamine had taken to him as some kind of protector. He thought Calamine was the one who done it."

Tyson pauses for a beat. "And what do you think, sir?"

Spragg leans forward and his voice drops a bit. If those eyes could see, they would be staring a hole through the Ranger. He says, "I don't think he's wrong."

*   *   *

Sunday dawns bright and beautiful, and Haddon is surprised to find himself actually wanting to attend church with the Eastons. Of course, he is given no choice in the matter, but it is good to *want* to go. Ada washed and ironed his clothes the night before, and although he doesn't have his suit, Ada finds an older, but handsome, vest of Lyman's and pins the back of it until it almost fits Haddon.

Now, in the wagon together, they trundle two or so miles to the little Baptist church that the Eastons helped establish some years ago. It has grown some since then, and that's good and bad. They always want more people to hear the gospel, but it is difficult to try to build friendships like the ones they already enjoy with new folks moving in, which they are doing by the truckload. Fort Worth is booming, and so is this little church, like it or not.

Haddon knows he should feel a little unsure here, with a bunch of new people who might want to know him more than he wants to be known. And yet, the setting is as familiar as his own skin. The whitewashed siding of the church, the open front door, the people filing in. It's like he always thought it could be, but never experienced. He knows the place. Well, not this place, but it might as well be this one, because he knows it like he knows his own dreams.

He follows a couple of steps behind the Eastons and watches them as they greet their friends and neighbors. He catches only snippets of conversation, but everyone seems to be glad to be there. Inside the church building, the same smell of oak pews and pine timbers floods Haddon's senses, and he feels like a baby in a crib. Lyman and Ada motion for him to join him on the second pew, next to the aisle. Everyone, of course, has their normal place, and if you aren't invited to sit in a particular spot, you may be asked politely to move. But Haddon is their guest, so he is welcomed.

The soft murmur of conversation dies down as a youngish man, not too much older than Haddon, steps up onto the stage and behind the pulpit. "Good morning," he says brightly.

The congregation answers in kind, but not all together like a formality. A smattering of

"Good morning, Brother Stockton," makes its way around the room. "Stand to your feet with me," he says, "as we open our hymnals to number three hundred twenty-two. Number three twenty-two..."

Everyone stands as the pianist plays a four-chord intro, then Stockton begins to keep time as he leads them in singing.

There is a fountain, filled with blood
Drawn from Immanuel's veins
And sinners plunged beneath that flood
Lose all their guilty stains

Haddon feels as if an invisible hand has reached into his chest and is tugging his heart right back through his skin. Lose all their guilty stains... It feels like the phrase has been burned onto his soul, but it's a good burn. He smiles, at first to himself, then at Ada as she notices the change in him.

Lose all their guilty stains,
Lost all their guilty stains
And sinners plunged beneath that flood
Lose all their guilty stains

After another hymn, a couple of older men fulfill their responsibility of passing the offering plate. When it comes by, Haddon gives generously. Ada smiles and rolls her eyes at his extravagance. Haddon feels a twitch in his soul, like a pinch to the side, when he suddenly remembers where the money came from. But the feeling passes, smothered by the joy of the day. After the offering, Brother Stockton takes the pulpit again.

"As some of you may have noticed," he says, "our pastor is not here today. Pastor Samuel took ill last night and is unable to get out of bed this morning. I'm sure you will join me in sending prayers his way. As it is, it was too short notice to get another preacher, so I thought we might open it up to you today. Does anyone have a testimony, or a word of encouragement from Scripture that they would like to share?"

Smiling faces politely turn this way and that, encouraging the other faces to say something if they want to. After a few moments of silence, a middle-aged woman with tight hair and a buttoned-up face raises her hand with some vigor. There is definitely something on her mind, which surprises no one. She stands before she is even recognized by Brother Stockton, who smiles stiffly and acknowledges her. "Yes, Mrs. Cooper?"

Mrs. Cooper doesn't just speak from her pew. She walks with great purpose to the front of the church and stands just in front of the pulpit, but at floor level, so as not to seem too impudent. "Well," she begins, "I certainly hope that we aren't going to *pay* the pastor for a day when he isn't working, but I suppose that is neither here nor there at the moment, though I hope the Pulpit Committee will take it under consideration. " She pauses and looks at each committee member in turn to make sure that they do just that. "Of course, I hope he feels better, as long as it wasn't something that he brought on himself." She pauses again, giving everyone time to infer whatever they like from that, and she doesn't seem to care much what they come up with. "Irregardless," she says, "I think it is high time that someone did something about the state of decency, or should I say *indecency*, that has pervaded our city. I mean, it's just shameful how—"

"Mrs. Cooper—" says Brother Stockton.

"—women can just walk around dressed however they like—"

"Mrs. Cooper—"

"—and the alcohol that is flowing through this city—"

"Mrs. Cooper!" It is not quite a shout from Stockton, but as close as you might hear in a Baptist church, at least this one.

Mr. Cooper sighs, but does not turn. "Yes?" she says.

"This," says Stockton, a little more controlled now, "is meant to be a time for reflection and testimony. I believe we can discuss the state of our city at another meeting. Thank you." Stockton waits to see if she gets the message and sits down, which she does, after too long of a moment. Stockton looks at the congregation. "Anyone else?" he says.

In answer, a frail, old hand rises slowly. Stockton smiles at the small woman and addresses her. "Yes ma'am, Mrs. Pate. Go ahead."

Mrs. Pate, deeply wrinkled and slightly stooped, stands with some difficulty, and turns to face the congregation. "Thank you, Brother Stockton," she says in a voice that trembles with age but carries the weight of a venerated matriarch. "I'd like to give a word of testimony." Warm smiles and nods encourage her to share her heart. "I just want to thank the Lord today," she says. A few "amens" come back to her from around the room.

"You see," she continues, "he saved me. Some of you may not know this, but the Lord Jesus saved me from being a slave to alcohol." A low rumble of surprise rolls through the crowd.

"He saved me from the foulest mouth you have ever heard on a woman." More stirrings, some of shock, some of intrigue.

"He saved me from the jailhouse." Now the

women instinctively lean back in their seats, and the men all lean forward. This is more information about Mrs. Pate than they have ever known before.

"He saved me from meanness"—this directly looking at Mrs. Cooper—"from violence, and from a life of crime." Gasps have become audible now. He even..." She examines the crowd. "Can you bear it? He even saved me from a life of prostitution."

Some of the murmurs have now become clear grumbles of offense. A couple of mothers are gathering their family's belongings and eyeing the door so as to protect their children's innocent ears. "And the most wonderful truth of all—" Mrs. Pate says, and the room falls quiet, all eyes and ears on her, "—is that the Lord Jesus saved me from all of those things... before I even had to experience them."

Mrs. Pate gives them a sly smile and goes to sit back down. As her meaning dawns on the people, their tension gives way to laughter and relief, with some more hearty "amens", and more than a few ladies fanning themselves.

Haddon has watched all of this as if entranced. He visibly stiffened when she spoke of a life of crime and hoped no one noticed. Now, though, it's as if he has just heard the greatest sermon that has ever been preached. A fire comes to life in his bones. Can he take the chance? He raises his hand.

Stockton is still smiling in relief when he nods to him. "Yes, young man?"

Haddon tries to swallow and can't, but he finds he has a voice anyway. "I have a word, if I may," he says.

"Of course," says Stockton.

Haddon naturally moves toward the platform as he speaks, not even aware of his own movement, but following a leading inside. He turns to the people in the church as he walks. "In the Gospel of John, chapter eight," he says, "Jesus found himself challenged with the task of sentencing a woman who was as Mrs. Pate just described. She had been caught in the very act of adultery. Think for a moment about what that means. Caught. In. The. Act." He pauses and watches them work that out and realize what he means. "The religious leaders of the day," he goes on, " wanted to condemn her, just as many of us might have thought of doing just a moment ago with this dear woman." He smiles at Mrs. Pate.

Now, just as natural as breathing, Haddon moves up on to the platform and toward the pulpit. He stops and looks at Stockton, though, waiting for permission. After all, this is neither his church nor his pulpit. Brother Stockton, though, just seems relieved to have someone take the service in what looks to be direction of some solid ground. Stockton steps aside and waves Haddon over. Haddon steps behind the pulpit and grasps its sides with his hands. This is the moment that he knew would someday come.

"But what makes us any better than the woman who stood before the Christ? That was his question to his audience then, and it is His question to us today..."

The spigot of his soul opens, and the words flow out like never before. At times, as he watches the faces of the congregation, open-mouthed, like hungry baby birds, he finds that he is almost watching himself preach at the same time that he is actually preaching, and he is duly impressed. He would not even correct someone today if they were to call him "reverend."

Haddon stands at the door of the church, just like the real pastor would if he were there, and shakes hands as the people leave. A woman takes his hand, beaming, and Haddon thinks he sees tears in her eyes. "That was wonderful, sir," she says, "just wonderful!"

A man, presumably her husband, follows right behind. "It certainly was," he says. "Pastor Samuel better get well quick if he wants to keep his position!" He chuckles and winks as he pats Haddon on the shoulder.

Another woman practically hugs him. "Wise beyond your years, young man," she says. "You are wise beyond your years. Where did you learn to preach like that?"

Haddon is humbly accepting the compliments, happy to his core that finally, someone is appreciating him for who he has always been. Preaching to a real church is very different from preaching to dull people or empty pews, and he feels the energy of it all surging through him. He is already thinking about what he will preach when he has another chance. He hopes it is soon. He has a lot of good sermons stored up. Even Ada and Lyman are bragging to everyone who passes by, that Haddon is staying with them.

At the edge of the crowd, though, a man stands alone under a tree, looking at Haddon and frowning. He is tall and thin, a little stooped in the shoulders, as if he has spent a lifetime bending at the waist. He has an unlit cheroot cigar in his mouth, and it is wet with the saliva of his concentration. As Haddon continues to field the well wishes and compliments, the man approaches Lyman, pulls him aside a few feet, and speaks to him in lowered tones. As soon as he can, Haddon politely disengages himself from the few people around him and goes over to join Lyman and the man. He can hear the conversation going on as he draws closer.

"...I'm sure there's nothing to it, Lyman," the man is saying. "I just... I don't know, I guess I just want to be sure..." As Haddon gets closer, both men notice him and Lyman waves him over.

"Haddon, come here, son," says Lyman. "This here is Mr. Hobbs, he owns a barber shop downtown near the stockyards. He says he might know you."

Haddon's smile changes from warm to cold in an instant. He has no idea what is back of this man's inquiry. "Is that so?" says Haddon. "I'm sorry, Mr. Hobbs, you don't look familiar to me at all."

Mr. Hobbs smiles, but it doesn't reach his eyes. "No, well, I wouldn't, would I?" he says. He takes the small cigar out of his mouth, turns his head, and spits a speck of wet tobacco off his tongue. "We have never met. You just look like someone I've seen before, is all. See, I have visited family from time to time in a little place called Black Ankle. Ever heard of it?" The cigar goes back in and his eyes narrow, waiting.

Haddon feels himself sway a little with the shock of hearing those two words, and he plants his feet firmly and speaks. "Yessir," he says. "Heard of it."

"Hm," says Hobbs. The cigar stays in his mouth and he speaks around it. "Seems there was some doings there recently, and somebody left town too sudden. My sister wrote to me about it."

Haddon tries to seem uninterested and polite, and he has never done anything so hard in his life. "Is that so?" he says. "Well, it was certainly nice to meet you, Mr. ... Hobbs, was it? Perhaps we will be seeing you again."

Haddon is sure that there are other noises happening around him, conversation, insects, horses—but at the moment all he can hear is a hum of trouble as the barber says, "Perhaps. Fine sermon, Reverend, uh... Chambers." He bows slightly to Lyman. "Lyman. Good day to you both." With that, he turns and walks away without a glance backward. It occurs to Haddon that no one today has said his last name before then.

Ada walks over to where Haddon and Lyman are still watching Hobbs leave. Lyman doesn't look like he is thinking on it too hard, and Haddon is trying to hide the fact that he is. "Gentlemen," says Ada as she slips her arm in Lyman's. "Sunday dinner will be ready very soon after we get to the house."

Haddon doesn't know if he will ever feel like eating again. "If you don't mind," he says, "I think that when we get back I'm just going to lie down for a little while. I'm not feeling very well."

Lyman frowns with worry. "You okay, son?"

"Yes," says Haddon a little too quickly, "yes, I'm fine. I'll be fine. Just too much... something."

"Well, alright," says Ada, "if you say so. It was awfully hot in that church and you sure preached with a lot of energy. I'll save some dinner for you in case you're hungry later. Do let me know if you need anything."

Haddon stretches out in the back of the wagon for the ride home. He looks and acts sick. Except it isn't an act.

* * *

At about the same time of day, in Black Ankle, Texas, Ranger Montgomery Tyson is sitting at the rough hewn kitchen table of a family with a hardscrabble farm down by the piney creek. He sits at the other end of the table from Joseph Chambers and his wife, Abigail. Joseph looks none too happy to have him there, but Tyson can't imagine the man has ever looked happy about anything.

Abigail says, "Are you sure I can't get you anything else, Ranger Tyson? I'm sorry there wasn't any supper left when you arrived. I don't cook as much as I used to when... when..."

Tyson lets the words trail off a little, then says, "No ma'am. Think nothing of it. This apple is fine." He pauses to shift the conversation. "So," he says, "help me understand. After your oldest boy died—"

"Was murdered," says Joseph.

Tyson starts again. "After Ethan was killed, you didn't see Haddon again after the next morning, when you saw him packing, ma'am?"

"That's right," says Abigail.

"Tell me," says Tyson, "is the name Calamine familiar to either of you?"

"Well, of course," says Abigail, "who could forget a name like that? His Christian name was Thomas, though, if I remember correctly."

"You knew him, ma'am?" says Tyson.

"Briefly, yes sir."

"How briefly?"

Joseph punches another sentence into the air. "Why you askin' about Calamine?"

"Well," says Tyson, turning the apple over in his hand, "seems he might be with Haddon. In fact, there's a chance that he might be the one responsible for the troubles that Haddon now finds himself in." He sets the apple down on the table.

Joseph hacks a harsh laugh, and there is loose phlegm in it. "Ain't likely," he says.

"Why do you say that, Mr. Chambers?"

Joseph looks like it is taking every ounce of resolve he can dredge up to talk about it. "After Hadd..." he says, then shakes his head. "I can't even say his name. After his Ma died, Calamine came over and befriended him. I had no interest in him anymore, so Calamine took it on himself to teach the boy how to shoot. He got pretty good at it, I reckon. Until..."

Tyson waits, but nothing comes next. "Until what?" he says.

"Until the day they went out to shoot and Calamine's gun blew up in his face," says Joseph. "All of fourteen years old. Damn shame."

Abigail jumps back in quickly. "It wasn't Haddon's fault," she says, "no one believed that. It was clear to all that the gun had blown up on its own. Those Colts are known to do that from time to time." She looks at Joseph and says, "It wasn't Haddon's fault."

Joseph glares at her and says, too loud, "He might not have pulled the trigger, but he was there all the same, and to my mind, that makes it his fault!"

Tyson's mind is busy for trying to assemble the pieces. "I take it," he says, "that Calamine was badly injured when the gun blew up, then?"

Joseph looks at Tyson like he must be slow in the head. "Injured?" he says. "You don't get it, Ranger. Calamine's been dead for years."

CHAPTER 11

It is dark outside of Lucas Easton's bedroom, and the sounds of a country night float in through the open window. Haddon is lying on the bed, still wearing his church clothes. He has been there all afternoon, not napping, not anywhere close to it, but thinking, or at least trying to. He is trying to figure something out, but he doesn't even know what it is or how to start.

He gets up from the bed, walks to the washbasin in front of the window, bends down, and splashes water on his face that has already been cooled by the night air. He reaches for a towel and dries his face, but as he lowers the towel, he sees something outside, half hidden in shadow, at the edge of the tree line—Calamine. Calamine looks at Haddon, smiles, steps back, and is swallowed by the black of the woods.

Haddon heard the Eastons go to bed some time ago, and now he hears Lyman's buzz saw snoring from behind the door at the end of the hall. If Ada can sleep through that, she certainly won't hear anything else. Haddon slips out of the bedroom, walks softly to the back door, and lets it shut silently behind him. As he nears the woods, he still can't see Calamine, but he hears his voice as if he is standing right next to him. "Been waiting a while," the voice says. "Glad you finally decided to look out your window."

Haddon steps into the shadows, too, and his eyes adjust enough to see Calamine leaning up against a tree a few feet away. "Why are you here?" says Haddon.

Calamine laughs, but not really. "I think you know why. We need to talk. And I think you know what about." Haddon says nothing, so Calamine continues. "Hobbs is going to ruin everything, you know."

"I don't know that," says Haddon, "and neither do you."

Calamine moves closer. "Yes, you do. You remember him. I do, at least. Hobbs doesn't just have family in Black Ankle. He used to work there, a few years ago. He cut your daddy's hair, and Ethan's too. You were younger then, and he might not have recognized you if it hadn't been for the news traveling about your brother."

"But that has nothing to do with me!" Haddon says. "It's you who should be afraid."

"Oh," says Calamine, "I don't want to be found, I surely don't. But let's not forget that, right now, it's likely *you* that the authorities want to find, not me. I can just as easily disappear. I've done it before."

"Listen to me," Haddon pleads. "Don't do anything. Mr. Hobbs is nothing. Nothing! He will forget about this!"

"Oh, don't worry, I won't lift a finger. You, however, need to at least know for sure, so that you aren't always looking over your shoulder at him."

"What am I supposed to do?"

"Just watch him for a little while," says Calamine. "Make sure he leaves this whole thing alone, which, like you say, he probably will. But if you don't take the time to know for sure, you will be living in fear far longer than you want to."

Haddon looks at the ground, still trying to work it all out. He turns and starts back to the house, then says, over his shoulder, "Just don't do anything."

"Oh," says Calamine, "you don't have to worry about me. Not at all."

On Monday morning, Haddon sits at his makeshift desk in the corner of the newspaper office. He has been trying to look busy for a couple of hours, but seeing nothing except the pictures moving across his mind's eye—images of Hobbs talking to a lawman, Haddon being arrested—and he can't even imagine what comes next. It's time to do something. He watches Lyman through his office window for another few moments, sees him immersed in someone's latest article, frowning and marking it up every few seconds. Haddon gets up and walks over to Lyman's office, gently knocks on the doorframe. Lyman looks up and waves him in.

"Yes, come in, son," says Lyman. "What do you need?"

"Well," says Haddon, "I had an idea for a story I would like to work on. There is some controversy brewing over in White Settlement concerning an Independence Day Parade. I'm going to ride over and feel it out."

Lyman nods. "It's your time and your dime, for now," he says. "If you feel like this is something worth looking into, go ahead."

"Thank you," says Haddon. "I'll see you at supper tonight." Haddon takes his hat and coat off the rack and steps out of the building.

Haddon does not have a plan. He pulls his hat down low over his eyes and saunters down

Main Street, stopping to look in a few shop windows along the way, but keeping his eye on the red and white barber pole down the street. He moves closer, walks across the street so he can look inside without being too obvious, and sees, through the front plate glass, that Hobbs is there. He is moving with scissors and brush around a customer, chatting and chuckling. Haddon steps back into the shadow of the building and waits.

An hour later, Haddon straightens, senses alert as Hobbs leaves his shop, turns around, and locks the door. Hobbs seems to be in a hurry, and moves off down the street. Haddon is reconsidering this whole thing when Calamine steps up behind him.

"I wasn't sure if you'd come," says Calamine, "so I been watching him."

After Haddon's heartbeat comes back down, he says, "Then I guess you've been staking me out, too."

"Well," says Calamine, "you looked a little shaky just now. I thought my being here might give you some courage."

"I'm fine," says Haddon.

Calamine nods down the street. "You're also losing him."

Haddon makes his decision, and strikes out

after Hobbs, staying across the street and behind him. Calamine is right there with him. In a few blocks, Hobbs arrives at the Western Union office and goes inside.

Ten minutes later, Hobbs steps out and looks around, then heads back in the direction that he came, in no particular hurry. Calamine leans up and whispers in Haddon's ear, "Well, that ain't good."

Haddon thinks on it. "Well, this doesn't help me any, just knowing where he went. I guess this was a wasted trip." He turns to leave, but Calamine plants a firm hand on Haddon's chest. "We need to see what he sent," he says.

"They won't tell me that."

Calamine smiles again, like a cat at a mouse hole. "Betcha they will," he says.

The front door of the Western Union office squeaks as it opens, and the telegraph clerk looks up to see who came in, then looks back down at the paper and pencil in his hand. Before the clerk can greet him, Haddon say, "Excuse me, but the man who just left... what did he send, and where did he send it?"

Without looking up again, the clerk says, "I can't tell you that, young man."

Haddon moves up to the counter. "It is very important to me to know what he sent," he says.

The clerk, still looking at his work, says, "And it is very important to me to keep my job."

Haddon is, for one of a few times, speechless. Calamine steps up and stands just behind Haddon's shoulder, raises his gun, points it at the clerk, and clicks the hammer all the way back.

At the sound, the clerk looks up, straight down the barrel of the gun. His resolve disappears like dust. He fumbles to bring the piece of paper in his hand up enough to read it. "He sent it to the Texas Rangers office," he says, quickly. "It says, HADDON CHAMBERS IS IN FORT WORTH. STOP. I KNOW WHERE HE IS STAYING. STOP. FIND ME AT HOBBS BARBER SHOP. STOP. THE OWNER."

The barrel of the gun is still inches from his face. Calamine lifts it up toward the ceiling and lets the hammer back down slowly.

Haddon finally lets out a breath. "That's all I needed," he says. Haddon turns to leave, and Calamine follows, revolver still in his hand.

CHAPTER 12

Supper in the Easton home is difficult, the atmosphere weighed down by a brooding Haddon Chambers. He is distracted, multiple emotions crossing his face one after the other—fear, anger, worry, fatigue—and he is only moving food around on his plate with his fork.

Ada decides she can't take it anymore. "Is something wrong with your dinner, Haddon?" she says. "Are your pork chops alright?"

Haddon comes back, but only for a moment. "What?" he says. "Oh... no, it's fine."

"It's just," says Ada, "that you haven't eaten a bite yet, and Lyman here is almost finished, though that's no surprise in itself—"

"I said it's fine!" The sudden burst from Haddon stills the room.

"Whoa, there, son," says Lyman, "there's no

call for that tone of voice. In this house you can raise a question and you can raise a doubt, but can never raise a hand or your voice. You understand?"

The young man sitting at the Easton's table now seems very unlike the one who they ate with Saturday night and took to church Sunday morning. The one here now is tight, frowning, and quick-tempered. "Who are you," he says to Lyman, "to tell me what I can or cannot raise? I am a grown and capable man, and I can make a life for myself, thank you very much!"

"Haddon," Ada pleads, "what has gotten into you?"

Haddon leans forward, volume and venom filling his words. "How dare you ask such a thing? My life is my business, and mine alone!"

Lyman's hand slams down on the table so that it rattles the dishes on the sideboard behind him. "That is enough!" he says. "No one speaks disrespectfully to my wife, not even me. You have done so twice now in as many minutes. You will hold your temper and your tongue, son."

Haddon's head swivels toward Lyman as if to take aim. "You know, you keep saying that," he says. "Calling me 'son'. I never agreed to be a stand-in for your dead son! I have... I..."

Tears spring to Ada's eyes as her hand goes to her mouth. It feels as though thunder is about to rumble. Lyman wipes his mouth with his napkin, folds it and places it next to his plate. He reaches over, squeezes her hand, and stands. "Ada, my dear," he says, "we will be back in a moment. Haddon... outside. Right now." Lyman doesn't wait for a response, just heads for the front door.

Haddon knows he has crossed a line, and part of him is sorry, but his emotions are too tangled. He stands, sulking, and follows Lyman out, down the porch steps, into the front yard. Lyman walks to a section of fence that they repaired together on Saturday. He leans on the top rail and looks off into the dying day. "Haddon," he says, "you don't get to where I am in the newspaper world without knowing how to see past the surface. What's going on? What has you acting like this?"

Haddon gives in and leans onto the fence, too, no more energy for anger. "I'm sorry, Mr. Easton. I am. But I have a problem you can't help me with."

"Well, we don't know that yet, do we?" says Lyman. "Tell me about it and let's see."

Haddon looks into the distance across the darkening fields, as if he is trying to remember and forget at the same time. "My hometown," he says, "is, in fact, Black Ankle, like Mr. Hobbs said. I recognized him. I left quickly a week ago because my brother was found shot dead, face down in a creek, and my father—if you can call him that—is trying to convince everyone that I did it." Lyman says nothing. "Well?" Haddon says. "Aren't you going to ask me? If I did it?"

Lyman shakes his head. "No," he says.

"Well, I didn't," says Haddon.

Lyman turns to look at him. "Do you know who did?"

"Yes," says Haddon, "and that is another problem."

"Tell me."

"Somehow," Haddon says, "I have acquired this kind of benefactor, a friend of his own choosing, my 'dread champion,' if you will. He has taken to me and taken on the job of protecting me, whatever he thinks that means."

"What's this friend's name?" asks Lyman.

"His name is Calamine."

"Look at me," says Lyman, and Haddon does. What he sees is not condemnation or shame, but real concern in his eyes and calm reason in his voice. "This Calamine is no friend. We need to go to the Sheriff tomorrow morning, Haddon. I'll go with you. You need to turn this Calamine fellow into the law."

Haddon takes a step back and sits on a stump beside the fence. "It's not that simple, Mr. Easton," he says. "There have been other...

incidents. To tell you the truth, I think that if it came down to it, Calamine would say that it was all me anyway, just to save his own skin. I can't take that chance."

"Well, then," Lyman says, "you need to send him away. Where does he stay?"

"That's a good question. He always just finds me. I suppose he tracks me, watches me. He could be watching us right now."

Lyman's gaze moves smoothly around the perimeter of his property, then looks at Haddon again. "Again, I tell you, Haddon, and mark my words: Calamine is no friend. If you see him again, you must make it clear to him that you will have no sympathy for him or his crimes any longer. Make him understand that he should leave you alone. Do you think you can do that?"

Haddon stands and tries to hold his head up, but it is heavier now than it has ever been. "Again, I don't think it's that simple, but... yes, I understand. When I see him, I 'll tell him."

"All right," says Lyman. "I'm going to go back in now. I suggest that when you are ready to come back inside, that the first thing you do is to apologize to Mrs. Easton. Don't worry, she is very forgiving. But she will only forget once she forgives." Lyman turns toward the house. "Good night, Haddon," he says.

"Mr. Easton?" says Haddon.

Lyman stops and turns toward him. "Yes?"

Haddon's head drops a little now, and he is glad that it has grown too dark for Lyman to see the shame in his face. "I do like it when you call me 'son'."

Lyman smiles. "Good night, son."

Haddon watches him go. "Good night," he says.

CHAPTER 13

Haddon is back at his desk at the office, going over the morning edition of the paper, trying to set his mind back to building a new life for himself. Mr. Easton is right. He has to make Calamine leave him alone. He looks up and sees someone in Lyman's office, but he can't see who it is. The man is tall and sinewy, and he moves and speaks with the slow grace of a wary mountain lion. The man hands Lyman a piece of paper. Lyman looks at it, turns it around as if to look for something on the back. Haddon realizes that Lyman is trying to show it to him through the window without looking like he is.

Haddon catches a glimpse, but it is enough. What he sees is a sketch. A pretty good one, actually. It is a sketch of Haddon's face on a WANT-

ED poster. Haddon stands, turns his back to Lyman's office, and crouches down as if to pick something off the floor. He pivots just enough to watch the man from the corner of his vision. Lyman turns the paper back over, frowns, and shakes his head as he hands it back to the tall man. The stranger shakes Lyman's hand, turns, and leaves the building. Haddon's gaze returns to the assistant editor's office, where Lyman catches his eye and jerks his head toward the back door. Lyman walks out the door, to the alley. Haddon counts to ten, and follows him.

In the alley, Lyman says, "Do you know who that was?"

"No," Haddon says, "I've never seen him before."

"Are you telling me the truth, son?"

"Yes!" says Haddon, "I swear to God, I have never seen him before in my life! Who was he?"

"That," says Lyman, "was a Texas Ranger named Montgomery Tyson. He has been following you and Calamine since a robbery and murder in a town called Birthright."

Haddon's legs give out and he sits hard on an old barrel in the alley. "Jesus," he says.

"He asked if you were staying with me."

Haddon looks up at Lyman. "And?"

"I couldn't lie to the man," says Lyman. Then a wry smile appears on his face. "At least not outright. I told him you had stayed with us, but you moved on. Don't know where you went."

Haddon's shoulders sag with relief. "Thank you," he says.

"Needless to say, though," says Lyman, "you can't come back to my house. I'll bring your things to you, but I will not put Ada in danger. You understand that, don't you?"

Haddon does not understand. He stands with speed. "What?" he says. "Where am I supposed to go? You just said that you told him I'm not there, so isn't that the perfect place for me to be?"

"Except," says Lyman, "that I'm not sure I was entirely convincing. Right now, I am the only lead Ranger Tyson has, and it is only a matter of time until he comes to visit me at home."

"Oh," says Haddon, bitterness rising in his voice. "I understand. Now that I'm trouble, you wash your hands of me."

"No," says Lyman, "that is not at all what I'm doing! I am trying to protect all of us, can't you see that?"

Haddon wants to argue with him, expose his hypocrisy, but in the same moment, the kindnesses that the Eastons have shown him flood his mind, and wrestle that desire down to the ground. The truth of what Mr. Easton has said sinks in. He knows he is on his own now. At least it was nice while it lasted.

"I'm sorry," says Haddon. "Yes sir, I understand. You and Mrs. Easton have been good to me when you didn't have to be. I don't want to involve you in this any further."

"I'm not going to just leave you on your own, Haddon," says Lyman. You just need to lay low for a while. Where will you go?"

Haddon takes a deep breath. "I still have the money I came to town with. I'll get a room at the hotel under a different name."

"Haddon," says Lyman, "I don't know what else to—"

Haddon lays a hand on Lyman's shoulder. "It's alright. Really, it is. I have to get out of this on my own, now, I think. Thank you for your kindness."

Haddon turns and walks away, rounding the corner onto the sidewalk, leaving Lyman alone, the alley as still as if he had never been there.

Mr. Hobbs has two customers in his barbershop. One is sitting in a barber chair in front of him, the other in a chair against the wall reading the newspaper. Haddon comes through the door, and a bell above him tinkles when the door hits it. Hobbs keeps cutting hair, and doesn't turn around. "Have a seat," says Hobbs around his soggy cigar stump, "I'll be with you in a while."

"I haven't come for a haircut," says Haddon.

Hobbs recognizes the voice and stops barbering, but looks at his customer as if sharing an inside joke. "Then you got no business here," he says.

Haddon takes another step in. "I need to speak with you," he says.

Hobbs goes back to cutting. "Go ahead, I suppose," he says.

Haddon's eyes take in the other two men. "Privately," he says.

Hobbs is incredulous and impatient. "I'm workin' here, boy! Besides," and he gives his customer a nudge with his elbow, "from what I hear, I don't think I want to be alone with you, anyhow."

Haddon takes another step. "That's the thing. What you've heard. It isn't true."

"It ain't, huh?"

"No, sir," says Haddon.

Hobbs finishes with his customer and brushes the hair off him. The man inspects himself in the mirror, pulls some coins out of a vest pocket, and puts them into Hobbs' hand. He makes no small talk as he makes a straight line for the door. The other man, by the window, folds up his paper and his unease, and follows him out of the door as the bell tinkles at their exit. Haddon and Hobbs are alone.

Hobbs shakes out the cape that had just been around the customer, and talks over the flapping of the cotton. "Look here, son—"

Haddon interrupts him before he can stop himself. "You don't get to call me that," he says.

A kind of steam settles onto Hobbs's expression. "Look... *BOY*...I know your family," he says. "I liked your daddy and your brother, and it's a damn shame what has happened." Hobbs stalks forward and Haddon backs up half a step. "Now I don't know everything, but I remember what your daddy used to tell me about you when I was cutting his hair. And that's when he mentioned you at all."

Hobbs isn't really moving toward him now, but his tall frame and stooped shoulders drive the force of his words forward. Haddon is backed up against another chair, with no further to go, and still, each word closes the distance.

"You daddy said," Hobbs went on without mercy, "that you was a weak little boy with a bad temper. He said you either couldn't or wouldn't do any real work around his place, and that either way, you was useless. He used to tell me that if you even lived past fifteen, that you weren't never gonna be nothing in this world." Something has dawned on Hobbs, now, though.

He tilts his head a little and barks a derisive little laugh in Haddon's direction. "Except that ain't quite right, is it? You've become a murderer pretty good, now, ain't you!"

Hobbs laughs harder now, but Haddon barely hears it over the ringing of his ears and the bell over the door as he runs outside, trying very hard not to throw up.

CHAPTER 14

Haddon half stumbles down Main Street, angry and dejected, only now thinking of the things he should have said to Hobbs. He steps onto the porch of the Fort Worth Hotel and walks through the ornate, etched-glass doors into the lobby. He rented a room here before going to see Hobbs so that he could gather his wits first. Now, as he stalks up the stairs, he realizes he has no wits left to gather again.

He opens the door to his room on the second floor, tosses his hat and gun belt onto the bedpost. He goes to the window, parts the curtains a little, and peers out. He looks down the street toward the barbershop, then up to the sky. Dark clouds are rolling in and thunder booms in the near distance. Haddon lies down on the bed, hands behind his head, staring at the ceiling.

He bolts upright at the sound of his door opening, reaches toward his holster, but sees that it is only Calamine coming in, closing the door behind him. "My goodness," says Calamine, "now who's itchy?"

Haddon gets up and walks to the window again, Calamine beside him, both looking out at the sky. "My, my," says Calamine, "there is most certainly a storm coming. Look at those clouds. They look like mourners mingling in a funeral parlor. Nothing good in that sky. Nothing at all."

Haddon paces the floor like a caged bobcat. "I have to talk to Hobbs," he says.

Calamine turns and leans on the windowsill, his arms crossed. "You just tried that," he says.

"I mean I have to talk to him again! Make him understand. I have to be more... more..."

"Of a man?" says Calamine.

"No!" Haddon says. "Of course not! I *am* a man!"

Calamine walks over and lies down on the bed, just as Haddon had done a moment ago, looking at the ceiling. "What you need to do," he says, "is remove him from the equation."

Remove him. Haddon knows exactly what that means. "No," he says. There is not much resolve in his voice.

"Yes sir, you do," says Calamine. "You need to go right back there and make sure that he can't tell no stories to no Rangers. *That's* what you have to do."

"I don't have to! I am a bigger man than that!"

Calamine closes his eyes and says, "No, you're not."

Haddon turns back to the window. "Shut up," he says. "He didn't mean anything by those things he said."

Calamine smiles, but it's a sad one. His eyes are still closed. "You just keep telling yourself that. But you ain't never gonna believe it."

Haddon has mustered all the false bravado he could find, but now he slumps into a chair in the corner of the room, his face in his hands. "Jesus," he says.

"No use talking to him anymore."

"I wasn't..."

Calamine waits a beat, then says, "I know." He sits up on the side of the bed and turns toward Haddon in the corner. "You have to do this, Haddon," he says.

Haddon looks up at him. "Tell me why."

Calamine explodes off the bed and stomps over to Haddon and leans directly over him, his voice booming like it is coming from a cavern. "Because you are not what he says you are!

I've been with you a long time, and I know! You might become it, though, if you don't face him down."

Haddon takes the lashing without resistance. "I know," he says.

The storm has passed over Calamine, but it continues to grow and growl outside. "Don't be scared, Haddon," he says. I'll be right there with you. I'm on your side."

Haddon takes a breath, stands up, grabs his hat and gun belt and puts them on before straightening his shirt. He reaches for the doorknob, but hesitates as if it might bite him when he grabs it. "I'm just going to talk to him," he says.

Calamine is close beside him. "I know," he says.

The clouds have let go of their cargo, and the rain is coming down in fat drops that leave nothing dry. Haddon and Calamine lower their hats and hunch their shoulders against the downpour, sloshing through the mud as they cross the street, unnoticed by everyone else doing the same. They arrive at Hobbs Barber Shop just after he has closed for the day. Haddon sees through the window that most of the lights are off, and Hobbs is sweeping up the hair beneath his chair, still chewing that same unlit cigar.

Haddon tries the knob. Hobbs hasn't locked the door yet. Haddon turns it, and he and Calamine walk in under the sound of the bell over the door. Hobbs turns at the sound as Haddon closes the door behind him. Hobbs sees who it is, and goes back to sweeping.

"Closed," Hobbs says.

"Yes sir, I know," says Haddon, from half shadow.

"Then what do you want?"

Haddon takes a moment to find his most firm voice. "I would like for you to apologize, sir."

Hobbs stops sweeping, looks at Haddon, laughs and coughs at the same time, shakes his head, and keeps sweeping. "Go home, boy," he says.

Haddon steps further in. "I ain't a boy anymore, Mr. Hobbs. And I am asking politely for an apology. That's all. Then I will leave."

Hobbs stops again but his hand clenches the broom tighter. His eyes narrow as he looks at Haddon with disbelief. His voice is low and rough, and the cigar never leaves his mouth. "Apologize? Hell," he says. "You want an apology? Fine." Hobbs stands the broom up against the chair, spits a bit of chewed tobacco leaf into the dirt pile, and steps toward Haddon. "Tell you what. You bring your daddy in here, and

I'll apologize to him. I'll tell him how sorry I am that his son ain't a splinter of the man he is." He steps closer. Haddon stands his ground this time, bowing up as best he can. "I'll tell him I'm sorry that he's got nobody of any account to carry on his name now that the good son is dead!" He slides to a couple of inches from Haddon, and Haddon can smell his wet, rancid tobacco breath. Hobbs is yelling now, and Haddon flinches as spittle peppers his face. "I'll tell him that I'm sorry that you ain't no more than a pimple on a coach driver's ass! But that's the only apology you will ever hear from me... *boy*... then I'm gonna get mad." Hobbs pushes his finger into Haddon's chest and shoves him with it. "Go home!"

Haddon takes a tentative step back. His breathing gets faster, and he tries to speak, but no words come. The fingers of his right hand twitch. In the same instant that lightning flashes outside the window, Calamine's hand whips up, and a shot explodes from his revolver, the boom of the gun in concert with the thunder. The bullet strikes Hobbs in the face, obliterating the cigar and everything behind it. The force of the bullet and the surprise of it pushes Hobbs backward, feet tripping over each other reflexively, and he lands and slides halfway through cheap green curtains into a supply room. Haddon looks at him, but no particular emotion surfaces. "Jesus, Calamine," he says. "What have you done now?"

Haddon and Calamine walk over to where Hobbs is still writhing somehow, clutching his shattered jaw. Haddon shakes his head sadly. "I just wanted to talk, Mr. Hobbs," he says. "Just talk."

Calamine extends his gun hand again and empties the revolver into the barber's head and chest until the hammer strikes empty chambers. Haddon uses his foot to shove Hobbs's legs behind the curtain. As the smoke from the gun curls upward and billows away, Haddon glances right and sees the name CALAMINE scratched into the barrel of the gun. They both turn and walk out the front door. Hobbs is still bleeding out when the bell over the door rings that second time.

CHAPTER 15

Last night's rain has moved east, but dark clouds still trail in its path, leaving the light in the Easton home dim and gray as Lyman finishes his breakfast and reaches for his tie. As he does, a knock sounds at the door.

"Good gravy," says Ada, "who can that be at this time of day? You expecting anyone, Lyman?"

"No," he says, "I'm not."

Ada opens the door to find a tall stranger with a bushy mustache, and a metal star in a circle pinned to his overcoat's lapel. "Yes sir," she says. "May I help you?"

The stranger removes his hat. "Yes, ma'am, you might," he says. "Are you Mrs. Easton?"

"I am."

"Is your husband still home?"

Lyman joins them at the door, his necktie loose at the top of his shirt. "I am here, Ranger," he says. "Ada, this is ranger Montgomery Tyson. Please, come in."

"Thank you," says Tyson, "I will. But first, I have to ask... is Haddon Chambers in the house or on your property?"

Ada looks at both men, becomes flustered, and steps back. Lyman says, "No, he isn't. Haven't seen him in days."

Tyson takes a hesitant step over the threshold of the home, looking all around as he does. "Yes," he said, "that's what you said yesterday. I just need to be sure."

"Then by all means," says Lyman, "come in and have a look around."

Lyman closes the door behind Tyson as he enters further, right hand hovering close by his holster. "Thank you," says Tyson.

"Ranger Tyson," says Lyman. "Has something happened?"

"Happened? Yes, I'd say so." He looks at Lyman as if to gauge his reaction to what he is about to be told. "Someone discovered the body of Mr. Hobbs this morning. He had been shot to death some time last night."

"What?" says Lyman. "Oh, my god..."

"You can imagine," Tyson continues, "my

urgency to know if Haddon Chambers is on your premises, then."

Lyman is surprised by the accusation. "What?" he says. "No, no, he couldn't . . . Haddon didn't murder Hobbs."

Tyson tilts his head. "He didn't?"

"No sir," says Lyman, "I don't believe so."

Tyson rubs his hand over the stubble of his beard. "Can you tell me who you think did murder him?" he says.

"It had to have been Calamine."

"Calamine, did you say?"

"Yes sir," says Lyman. "You see, Haddon told me about him for the first time yest... before he left. Apparently, Calamine has attached himself to Haddon as some sort of obsessed hanger-on who sees himself as Haddon's best friend and defender. If he felt Hobbs was a threat to Haddon in any way, well..."

"And what makes you think Calamine would do something like this?" says Tyson.

"Well," says Lyman, "Haddon believes he has done it before, on his behalf, if you will. His brother, for one. And then he mentioned another 'incident' in a town east of here—"

"Birthright."

"Yes, that's it. Birthright."

"Hm," says Tyson. "May I see the room where Haddon stayed?"

"Certainly," Lyman says, "it's right this way." Lyman leads the lawman to the other bedroom and opens the door. Tyson enters and walks carefully around the room, looking at everything. "This belonged to our son, Lucas," says Lyman. "We lost him some time ago."

"I'm sorry," says the ranger, and he means it. Tyson stops and examines the map on the wall. "Is this a map of a real place?" he says.

"Yes," says Lyman, joining him at the map. "That is my fishing cabin at Mineral Wells. Our son drew that when he was a little boy, but it is amazingly accurate. He loved it there. He's buried there."

Lyman can tell that now the gears are turning behind Tyson's eyes. "Did Haddon know about that cabin?" he asks. "Did he ever ask about this map?"

"Yes," says Lyman, "I believe Ada mentioned that he had asked about it."

"Hm," Tyson grunts. "Well," he says, "right now this cabin is the only lead I have for which direction Haddon and his friend Calamine might have gone." The ranger turns to Lyman, decision made. "I am going after him, Mr. Easton. May I borrow your map? I know it's very special to you, but it's all I have."

"No," says Lyman. "You may not borrow it."

"Mr. Easton," says Tyson, "there are some

things going on here that you don't understand—"

"Then you can explain it to me on the way,"
says Lyman. "You won't need the map, because
I'm going with you."

*   *   *

Haddon and Calamine have ridden west
from Fort Worth, stopping only to water and
rest their horses. After some time, they pass a
small wooden sign by the dusty road that says,
"Mineral Wells, TX". They ride on, up into the
hills, across a bridge spanning the Brazos River,
brown and shallow at this point. Haddon stops
for a moment to get his bearings. He looks to his
right and sees a path, almost covered by scrub
brush, but still there. He goads his horse into
it. At the end of the path, they arrive at a small
cabin, just a shack, really. A sign nailed to the
front door says *Easton West*. "This is it," says
Haddon.

The men dismount, take their horses to a
nearby water trough, and find them feed in another small shack a few yards away. There is an
old padlock on the door of the cabin, and Calamine shoots it apart with ease. Haddon pushes
the door open and they step inside the gloom
and dust of better, happier years.

There are two beds in the small cabin which don't look to have been used for some time. There is still just enough daylight for Haddon to find a kerosene lamp and some matches in a cabinet. The lamp still has some fuel in it. Haddon strikes one of the matches, sets the flame to the wick, and replaces the glass as a glow fills the room. Now he can see there are cans of beans and peaches on a shelf. Calamine takes his knife to the lid of a can of peaches and Haddon lies down on the bed and tries to unravel what has become his life.

Haddon says, "It's over, Calamine."

Calamine pries cut metal from the top of the can and stabs a piece of a peach, then transfers it to his mouth. Slurping the sweet juice from around it, he says, "What's over?"

"All of it," says Calamine. "The killing. The running. My own damn life."

Calamine walks over to the bed and stands over Haddon. "I'll tell you when it's over," he says. "The killing. The running. The life."

Haddon frowns at him. "What does that mean?"

"It means what it means, friend Haddon Chambers," says Calamine. He steps across the room and stretches out on the other bed. "But right now, I'm tired. And if you don't mind, I am going to sleep the sleep of the innocent."

Haddon looks at him across the room. "You are far from innocent," he says.

Calamine smiles as he lays back and lowers the brim of his hat over his eyes. "All how you look at things, Reverend," he says. "All how you look at things."

Haddon waits for more from Calamine, but nothing comes. He settles in, but sleep doesn't come. He just keeps an eye on Calamine.

CHAPTER 16

Haddon jolts awake with the feel of a cold gun barrel pressed to his forehead. It takes him a few breathless seconds to realize that he was dreaming. He looks across the room, and sees that Calamine is not in the other bed. Through the window, Haddon sees the lightening sky that is just before sunrise. It bolsters his hopes that the darkest part of the night is over.

He gets out of bed, still dressed from the night before, and walks outside. He walks over to a bluff, an outcropping of rock that overlooks the Brazos River winding a hundred feet below. Cactus and scrub brush surround his feet, but the view from here is breathtaking. Haddon yawns, stretches, and looks out over the valley. Just across the river, a dozen wild turkeys strut into a pasture, the orange cast of the morning haze brightening their tail feathers. He looks around and behind him again. Calamine is not in sight.

Some fifty feet behind Haddon, mostly hidden by the low brush and the shadows of changing light, Montgomery Tyson and Lyman Easton ease up on the path to the cabin. Tyson is in front, gun drawn. As the sun adds more light to the morning, they see Haddon standing ahead of them, looking out over the edge of the bluff. He is wearing his gun belt, and the holster is definitely occupied.

"Stay here," Tyson whispers, "I'm going up there."

Lyman touches his elbow to stop him. "No," he says, "if he sees you first, there's no telling what he might do, out of pure fright. He needs to hear my voice."

Before Tyson can object, Lyman steps out from cover and walks to the corner of the cabin. "Haddon?" he says. "Son?"

Haddon flinches, his right hand flying to the gun in his holster as he turns, but he doesn't draw.

"Don't come any closer, Mr. Easton!" he says. "I mean it!"

Lyman holds both hands out in front of him.

"It's alright, Haddon. I had to come and find you."

"Why?" says Haddon.

"Because I don't want you to be alone. Remember that ranger who was looking for you?"

Haddon's hand presses down on the handle of his gun. "Yes..."

"I convinced him to try and let me help you. Can I have him come out?" Lyman doesn't wait for an answer. "Tyson? Come join me."

"No guns!" says Haddon.

Lyman speaks over his shoulder. "No guns, Tyson."

Tyson steps out and walks slowly to where Lyman is now standing no more than thirty feet from Haddon. Tyson's gun is holstered.

"Tell him to throw his gun over in the bushes!" says Haddon.

"I can't do that," Tyson says. "But I will keep it here, in its holster, until I talk to Calamine. I need to talk to Calamine, Haddon. Can you help me do that?"

Haddon relaxes a little and nods. "Well," he says, "it's a good thing you found me first. Calamine doesn't care much for conversation."

"Then let me talk to him, son," says Tyson. "Your friend is gonna get you killed one day, and I'll tell you right now, you're better off without a friend than you are dead."

Haddon looks at Lyman with sad eyes. "You know," he says, "all I ever wanted was for someone to tell me I was a good man. That I was going to be worth something some day. My father should have told me that, shouldn't he? Why couldn't he tell me, just once... just once... that I was a good son?"

No one has an answer for him. They all seem to know that it can't be answered, not really. Haddon turns, his head down, to go look for Calamine. As soon as he steps into the brush, Calamine bursts out, fast and silent, like a pit viper. He raises his right hand, and the gun fires.

Tyson couldn't get his hand around his weapon fast enough, but he dodges to the side just enough for the bullet to gouge a trough out of the right side of his scalp. The impact and pain sends his gun flying from his hand, over the edge of the bluff.

Haddon stares in shock as Calamine swings the gun left and centers it on the chest of Lyman Easton, who is frozen in his steps. Calamine levels the iron sights to his shooting eye and smiles. "Say hello to Lucas for me," he says.

In that fraction of a moment, something breaks inside of Haddon. Lyman's death is one too far, and Haddon would not be able to live with it. "No!" he shouts, as he lunges toward Calamine and grabs his outstretched arm. The gun goes off just as Haddon pushes the trajectory up past Lyman's head. Haddon wraps himself around Calamine's arm and pushes him to the ground, falling on top of him.

But as Haddon lands, he doesn't feel the muscle and flesh of Calamine under him. He only feels cold, rock hard dirt. Then he sees something that confuses him even more. The arm that he is holding down, the arm that holds the Colt .45, warm and smoking, is his own. In its barrel is scratched a name, deep and well grooved: CALAMINE.

There is no one else on the ground with him. Somewhere, in the distance, he hears Lyman's voice, as if from a well.

"Jesus, Haddon," he says. "What have you done, son? What have you done?"

Another voice moves into his head. It's Old Man Spragg. *You let the wolf in, son... he done the rest.*

Haddon is paralyzed on the dirt. "No..." he says. Then he is instantly transported to Thrush Creek late at night, where he sees his brother Ethan rise from the fence that he has been working on, looking into the trees. *Daddy, is that you?*

Haddon feels the gun explode and watches as his brother's body twists backward to lie face down in the creek.

"No..." he says again, with more pain laced in it now. Haddon can't take his eyes off the gun in his hand. Abigail speaks to him. *I forgive you...*

Then it is Spragg again. *The wolf, it feeds on certain things. Jealousy. Pride. Anger. Murder in the heart...*

The scene in Haddon's mind changes, and he is staring down the barrel of the gun at the banker in Birthright. *Mister, please... I don't care who you are... please...*

Haddon hears his own voice now. *Take off your nightshirt...* Another explosion, and the banker is twisted and silent on the ground in front of him.

Then Haddon is standing in front of a terrified clerk at a Western Union office. The clerk is wide-eyed, Haddon's reflection in them, gun leveled.

Now the whole scene swirls around Haddon again, and he is in Hobbs' barber shop. *He said you was a weak little boy with a bad temper... You've become a murderer pretty good now, ain't you...* And then Hobbs' face explodes, and Haddon lowers the gun and empties the rest of it into him. *I just wanted to talk, Mr. Hobbs,* he hears himself say. *Just talk...*

The day is now dawning on Haddon on that bluff in Mineral Wells, along with the realization of what he has done. He gets to his feet, swaying, the .45 heavy in his hand. "Oh, god, no," he says. "Oh, Jesus..."

Haddon is suddenly aware that his right arm is sore, with a deep and stabbing pain. He rolls his shirt sleeve back and sees, carved into his forearm with an old pocket knife, the letters of a name that matches the barrel of his gun: *C-A-L-A- and so forth*. And he hears his tormentor's voice again. *I'm always on your side, Haddon... always on your side...*

Then, the Calamine in his head says the only thing that makes sense. *I'll tell you when your life is over...*

Haddon looks up, dazed, and sees Tyson stirring on the ground, wounded but alive. He sees Lyman staring at him, unbelieving. And he knows that he cannot bear to see disappointment in someone's eyes again, not for a moment longer. He sinks to his knees there, on the edge of the bluff, overlooking the rising sun on the Brazos. He raises his old friend, Calamine, and puts the barrel up against his forehead.

"Sufficient unto the day," he says, "is the evil thereof."

As his finger begins to tighten on the trigger, the first tears that he has felt since the night his mother died rise to his eyes. "Mr. Easton?" he says.

"Yes?" says Lyman softly.

"Could you call me 'son' again?"

"Haddon," says Lyman. "Son... my boy... Will you let me come to you?"

Haddon's tears break the dam of pain that has held them back for so long. He nods, and the gun drops from his hands onto the packed dirt. Lyman walks over, kicks the gun away, kneels down, and takes Haddon in his arms.

"It's alright, son," he says. "It's alright. I will be with you now, no matter what. I won't leave you."

The deer in the field across the meadow and the turkey buzzards gliding on the rising warm air above are oblivious, and always will be, to the magnitude and pain of the scene before them.

EPILOGUE

Spring has brought colorful blossoms to the cactus and other brush lining the path to *Easton West* in Mineral Wells. Today, Lyman and Ada Easton walk another path, away from the cabin, that leads to a small green plot of grass under the shade of a mesquite tree. In that plot stands a weathered grave stone that reads:

LUCAS EASTON
GONE TOO SOON
BELOVED SON
IN OUR HEARTS FOREVER

Lyman and Ada hold hands and gaze at the grave of their son, as they always do when they visit, each remembering their time with him.

Beside that one is another marker, a newer one, a wooden cross. Lyman reaches into a bag that he has brought and removes a freshly engraved plaque for the marker. As he pulls it out, his fingers brush a piece of paper next to it. He takes the paper and unfolds it, knowing what it is. It's a letter that Haddon had written, that he was allowed to read to them before the gallows floor dropped from under him. Lyman reads the words again:

Dear Mr. and Mrs. Easton,

I want you to know that I accept this day. I own what I have done. I would like to think that I can blame someone else. A father, a brother. A ghost. But no. The things for which I am here today, those things were done by my hand.

But I'm alright. Because I lived long enough to know what love feels like. Mr. and Mrs. Easton, there is something that I have never said to another human being in my whole life. It is fitting that it be the last thing I ever say: I love you, too.

Lyman flinches at the memory of the clunking sound that the trapdoor made. Neither he nor Ada kept watching. They weren't there to see Haddon hang, they were there so he wouldn't feel so alone.

Lyman takes the plaque and hangs it on a nail driven into the top part of the cross. He steps back and he and Ada admire it.

"You did good, sweetheart. It looks very nice," says Ada.

"Well," says Lyman. "I just thought it might be nice to always have over him the words he so longed to hear." He thinks for a moment. "You know, as far as I'm concerned, Haddon Chambers was murdered. Murdered by a cold-blooded killer."

Ada steps forward and lays flowers on both graves. Before they walk away, Lyman takes a moment to read the inscription on the plaque again.

HADDON CHAMBERS
A GOOD PREACHER
A GOOD MAN
A GOOD SON

As they make their way back down the path, Lyman hears an echo of the refrain from the hymn they sang in church with Haddon that day:

Lose all their guilty stains,
Lose all their guilty stains
And sinners plunged beneath that flood
Lose all their guilty stains.

ACKNOWLEDGMENTS

In July of 2016, I decided I wanted to learn how to write a screenplay. This was a few months after the release of the second album from The Mulligan Brothers, *Via Portland*. Listening to that album, I was struck by the sheer brilliance of one song in particular: "Calamine". As soon as I heard it, a story began to unfold in my head, and I knew that it would be a great premise for a movie. I bought a book or ten on screenwriting, and got to work, hoping that the songwriter, Ross Newell, wouldn't mind very much if I eventually landed an Academy Award® on his idea.

Partly out of respect and partly out of fear of being sued, I took Ross the finished first draft. Turns out, Ross Newell is a supremely kind and humble rock star, and he loved it. After some time, we had the opportunity to morph the screenplay into a stage play, which debuted at the Mobile Theatre Guild in Mobile, Alabama on September 6, 2019. The response was happy and gracious, and it gave me reason to think that the story might have the bones of a novel inside of it, too. And, what do you know, here it is in your hand.

There are so many people to acknowledge for the existence of this book, not least of all, the cast and crew of CALAMINE the stage play, especially Board President David Doolittle, who opened up the doors and the curtains to this unknown playwright with an untested story. Then again, we grew up together, so he kind of had to do it.

I also need to thank my family for enduring not only every draft of this danged thing since 2016, but also their tireless efforts in helping to stage the play. On top of that, my wife, Mary Ann, and son, Nathaniel, proofread and added priceless suggestions to an early draft of the novel.

The greatest thanks, though, are unsurprisingly reserved for my favorite singer/songwriter, Ross Newell. Ross not only approved the script, but he showed up for every rehearsal when he wasn't on tour, and performed at every show. I have pictures of him in his stockinged feet painting the stage black the night before our first show. The most valuable thing that I have received from this entire process is becoming friends with him. And, just so everybody knows, I am not nearly finished capitalizing on his talent for my own ends.

With that, I hope you enjoyed this story. If there are any mistakes—blame Ross. It was his idea to begin with.

Mark Wyatt
Mobile, Alabama
May 2020

ABOUT THE AUTHOR

Mark Wyatt is an author, a playwright, an award-winning actor and producer, and a publisher. Mark holds Bachelor's and Master's degrees in Communication and a Ph.D. in Biblical Studies. He lives in Mobile, Alabama with his wife, Mary Ann, and whichever of his four children are still at home. When he isn't writing or working as a hospice chaplain, you will probably find him either reading in a hammock or kayaking on the neighborhood lake.

Calamine is his first novel. He is currently at work on his next novel, while continuing to develop ideas for more stories from Ross Newell murder ballads.

Mark can be reached through wyattpublishing.com. Follow him on Facebook and at drmarkwyatt.writer.wordpress.com, which he sometimes updates, but not nearly enough.

Includes the song, *Calamine*

Includes the live version of, the
song, *Calamine*

FOR ROSS NEWELL MUSIC, MERCHANDISE,
TOUR DATES AND MORE, GO TO
WWW.ROSSNEWELL.COM.

ALSO, FOLLOW HIM ON FACEBOOK AND
PATREON!

You have a story.
We want to publish it.

Everyone has as a story to tell. It might be about something you know how to do, or what has happened in your life, or it may be a thrilling, or romantic, or intriguing, or heartwarming, or suspenseful story, starring a cast of characters that have been swimming around in your imagination.

And at Wyatt House Publishing, we can get your story onto the pages of a book just like the one you are holding in your hand. With professional interior design and a custom, professionally designed cover built just for you from the start, you can finally see your dream of being an author become reality. Then, you will see your book listed with retailers all over the world as people are able to buy your book from wherever they are and have it delivered to their home or their e-reader.

So what are you waiting for? This is your time.